FOR THE LOVE OF A WIDOW

Christina McKnight

La Loma Elite Publishing

Dedication
For Jason, my brother, a US Navy veteran~

I know the sacrifices of servicing your country firsthand
from you.
Your personal dedication to our country has always
inspired me to find my
own way to make the world a better place.

Prologue

London, England
May 1808

Thump, thump, thump.

Daniel brushed his knuckles against his palm as he glanced down at his attire and hastily smoothed his hands over his rumpled coat. The movement caused him to sway slightly as he steadied his stance.

"*Hiccup.*" Blast it all, but he despised ending his afternoon entertainments early to accompany Lady Lettie to yet another overly crowded ball, only to stand forgotten while she spoke, laughed, and danced late into the night. He'd done his best to avoid several afternoon entertainments over the last fortnight, including a garden party and a musicale recital.

The woman was his betrothed. She should, at the very least, see to him before wandering off to socialize with the other debutantes making their grand coming out in London.

It was exceedingly possible Lettie wouldn't notice his less than proper garb or his tardy arrival.

Thump, thump, thump. He pounded the door once more as a resounding pain moved from his clenched fist and up his arm to settle in his stiff shoulder.

Could it be that Lord and Lady Percival, with their daughter in tow, had already departed for the soiree when Daniel didn't arrive at the requested time?

He sniffed. It would be his luck to have disentangled himself from the lovely, raven-haired opera singer and dealt with her wrath, only to hurry to Carrolton Hall to find that his evening obligations and presence were no longer needed.

Which was in line with how Daniel had felt of late: unneeded, unwanted, and thoroughly disposable. His man of business and estate stewards at his various properties had no use for his attendance to keep his residences and business ventures turning tidy profits.

Leaving Daniel to spend his time—and money—however he saw fit.

The thought sparked an idea. If he turned around now, maybe he would arrive at the Theatre Royal on Drury Lane before the enticing Mademoiselle Sabine saw fit to dress for her evening upon the stage.

His hopes of escaping another tedious evening in Lady Lettie's shadow crashed when the Percival butler opened the door and gestured for Daniel to enter. He knew it was petty of him to blame Lettie for the absolute crush she was making during her season—and the attention it took off him—but he was annoyed by it all.

"This way, your grace." The servant stepped to the side, allowing Daniel entrance. "My lord and the duchess are finishing their meal before departing. They are expecting you." The servant's words ran together as he inspected Daniel from head to toe. His pinched expression told him that the butler found him lacking—in more ways than one.

Bloody hell, but Daniel wasn't in the habit of allowing a mere butler to cast judgment on his person. He stumbled across the threshold and into the foyer before following the man toward the dining hall. Another hiccup escaped, and Daniel pressed his hand to his mouth to stop the next.

He should have sent his regrets for the evening and stayed tightly in the willing arms of Sabine, his latest attraction—or was she a *distraction*? Yet beyond his own servants, Daniel hadn't another soul to call friend. Lettie, or Lady Collette as she was known by the *ton*, was his oldest and dearest friend. When their childhood acquaintance had changed from friendship to courtship and eventually an official betrothal, was when Daniel had lost interest in it all. Odd that it was at the same time that Lettie was no longer his hidden gem, but polished and presented to society…taking her place as a diamond of the first waters.

He was more than a pet to be led around on a leash, no better than a basset hound, or a bauble pinned to her hat piece.

No longer were they children with the freedom to scurry about their respective homes or climb the plum trees in Daniel's London garden—no, this year, Lettie had been introduced to society and needs must act with the decorum and grace expected of a future duchess.

His future duchess.

He laughed at the notion—Lettie was to be a duchess with or without her marriage to Daniel.

Lady Percival held one of the few English Dukedoms that had been granted letters patent to pass to a female relation if a male heir did not exist.

Daniel stumbled on unsteady legs as he waited for the butler to open the door to the dining hall. His chance to flee had passed.

The servant didn't hesitate, but pushed the door wide and announced in a clear, crisp voice, "The Duke of Linwood, my lord."

"Linwood!" Lord Percival boomed. "You are late."

"My—" *Hiccup.* Bloody hell, could he not keep his body under control? "Apologies." Maybe he should have taken the time to stop at his home and change into evening attire with a neatly tied cravat—and possibly allowed the spirits dulling his senses to subside—before arriving at Lettie's home. "I fear the day slipped me by, my lord."

"It is too bad you did not allow the scotch to do the same," Lady Lettie said under her breath with a snort.

Daniel turned a glare in her direction. Her plum pudding sat forgotten on the table as her stare narrowed on him. Her soft brown hair was upswept and piled high atop her head, the candlelight from above glistening off its shiny, pinned curls. He knew if the pins were removed, her hair would hang in waves to the middle of her back. The sight of her never ceased to take his breath away. Unfortunately, her scowl did naught but remind Daniel of his tardiness and unacceptable attire.

"Barclay," Lady Percival shrieked, motioning for the footman to remove her plate. "What is that dreadful stench?"

Daniel took a tentative sniff at the room, but smelled nothing amiss. The lingering aroma of duck soup and pheasant was all that was recognizable.

A footman pulled out the chair beside Lettie, and Daniel moved to his place, all but falling into the waiting chair as his mind whirled.

"Port, your grace?" the servant asked as he placed a plate of plum pudding before Daniel.

The thought of eating anything made his stomach roil. "No, thank you." He waved the servant off.

Reluctantly, Daniel glanced to his right at Lettie. She stared at her plate but made no move to pick up her utensil, or address him after her initial snide remark. Her brow was pinched, and her lips pressed together in a frown. He wanted to inquire as to what he'd done to irk her or deserve her avoidance at present.

"My heavens. The stink is growing!" Lady Percival retrieved her kerchief from her sleeve and waved it before her face before pressing it to her nose. "What in all of creation is Cook doing?"

"It is not Cook, Mother," Lady Lettie mumbled, picking up her fork and pushing the pudding around on her plate, but still she made no move to take another bite.

"Then what is it?" Percival demanded.

Lettie cocked her head in Daniel's direction and let one simple word free. "Him."

Daniel chuckled. "I assure you, my lady, it is not I." Lord and Lady Percival turned to scrutinize him as if noting for the first time that his jacket looked to have been trampled by a herd of livestock before Daniel had slipped it on. "Verily, I smell nothing out of the ordinary."

If he'd known he was to face an inquisition, Daniel wouldn't have turned down the glass of port.

It was Lettie who exhaled next. "Your grace, you reek of scotch and"—she paused, leaned ever so slightly toward him, and breathed in a shallow sniff, her nose immediately wrinkling as she recoiled— "and… is that lemon verbena?"

Daniel pulled the lapel of his coat to his nose.

Ah, lemon verbena, the intoxicating perfume of Mademoiselle Sabine.

He glanced back to Lettie, who now leaned as far away from him as possible, her arms crossed and a knowing look in her eyes.

Could she know of Daniel's mistress?

If Sabine could ever be called such by any one man. He'd only met the opera singer a fortnight before, and after a particularly trying evening watching man after man place their name upon Lettie's dance card, Daniel had given in and sent a note, requesting for Sabine to join him for a meal the following night.

Instantly, the songstress filled the place Lettie had always been meant to fill, the void left after his father's death the year before—his mother having succumbed many years prior. He'd begun to look forward to afternoons and nights spent at the woman's quarters off Drury Lane and not utterly alone in his townhouse with only servants for companionship—or following in Lettie's wake like a besotted fool.

"Mother, Father." Lettie stood, and the footman quickly pulled her chair back. "I have something I need to discuss with the pair of you—oh, and your grace, as well."

A spot of unease prickled the hairs at the back of Daniel's neck at her formal request.

Her chin tilted up with confidence; however, her hands shook slightly as they wrung her dinner serviette.

"Certainly, my daughter," Barclay said. "What is it?"

Her face paled and took on an unfamiliar green tone. "I wish to end my betrothal to Lord Linwood."

"What?" the duchess screeched, her high-pitched voice causing Daniel's head to pound.

"Colette, what is this about?" The earl set his utensils aside and stared up at his only child, his brow pulled low in question. "You and Daniel have been promised to one another since childhood."

"Do not be silly, girl," Lady Percival said. "Sit down and finish your pudding. The carriage will be brought round shortly, and we will be off. An evening outside this house will do you good—clear your head, as it were."

Daniel had never questioned the duchess's ability to act as if another hadn't spoken, but it was only reinforced when the woman retrieved her spoon and bent over to steal a bite of pudding from her husband's plate.

"I will not be going." Lettie's voice echoed in the cavernous room, silencing the scrape of the duchess's spoon as it took a second swipe at the earl's pudding. "Daniel, please inform my parents that you do not wish to marry me."

"I—" All thought evaporated as Daniel sat up straight, glancing between Lettie and her parents, his

7

liquor-addled mind clearing. Their families had settled on the match years ago. It wasn't something he'd ever questioned; only saw it as an inevitable occurrence in his future. Daniel had no issues with Lettie or their betrothal. Though a tad idealistic, Lettie was poised, graceful, and witty. All things he'd been raised to desire in a wife. That she was also beautiful did not go unnoted.

"Tell them, Daniel," she demanded, turning to stare down at him.

"I, well, I cannot admit that I have ever pondered the notion of *not* wedding you, Lady Lettie." It had been his late father's dying wish: that Daniel solidify his betrothal to Lettie, forever joining the two families for generations to come. "Let us discuss—"

"I have met another I wish to marry."

Her confession landed heavier than a rock in the pit of Daniel's stomach.

Met another? When, he wanted to demand. How? And especially, whom?

"I am in love with another, and we plan to wed, with or without your approval." Lettie stood a bit taller, and Daniel sobered quickly, his pride in her growing, even though giving her what she sought meant he'd be losing the final stable thing in his miserable existence. "Within a week's time, I will marry Mr. Gregory Hughes, and we shall depart London—all of England, in fact."

"This is absurd, Barclay." The duchess turned to her husband, pleading for his support. "Tell her that this will not be happening. Heavens, I do not even know a Mr. Gregory Hughes!"

The earl's mouth hung open in shock as he moved his attention from his wife to his daughter, and back once more.

"The man is after her dowry, I presume." Lady Percival shook her head from side to side. "I will not allow it."

Lettie took advantage of her father's stunned silence to continue on her course. "Lord Linwood, please inform my parents you are willing to forgo our families' agreement, thus freeing me to wed Gregory."

Who in the bloody hell *is* Gregory, Daniel wanted to demand; however, he risked a glance at Lettie then, and any rebuff he'd planned slipped from his mind. He may very well be deep in his cups—and smelling of another woman—but he bloody well knew when a woman was telling the truth. Her look pleaded with him to do as she asked.

He hesitated still.

Lettie was—had *always* been—the one constant in his ever-changing life. No matter where he went, no matter what he did, he always knew she'd be waiting for him.

The last year had tested their relationship, as Lettie had been introduced to society, and Daniel had fallen deeper and deeper into despair and loneliness— ultimately taking to his club and other unsavory activities.

If he agreed to break off their betrothal, it would bring disgrace upon both their families. It did not bother Daniel to live in such a shadow of ill-repute, but never would he allow anyone to think poorly of her.

"Are you certain this is what you want?" he asked. When she only nodded, Daniel continued, "You love this man?"

"Gregory, his name is Gregory—and I *do* love him, very much so."

"He will treat you well, provide for you?" Daniel could not believe he was entertaining the idea of giving in to her demands. "He has the means necessary?"

She nodded again.

"I certainly hope he does because you will not see a single schilling from your father or me if you continue down this unacceptable path, young lady." The duchess stood abruptly, tossing her napkin onto the table before turning a pointed stare to Daniel. "And if you think to go along with this ruse, Lord Linwood, you will depart this house immediately."

Daniel lumbered to his feet, surprised his balance had returned. "I bid you all ado and good evening."

He gave a curt bow to Lady Lettie and started for the door.

It wasn't until he'd made his way down the hallway toward the foyer Daniel sobered to the realization that his life—the life his parents had planned for him—and the future he'd always counted on, thought to be his due, was gone. Forever out of reach.

"Blast it all," Daniel muttered.

Though Lettie had chosen another, he was not without distractions of his own.

A jaunt to Drury Lane was exactly what a night such as this called for.

Chapter One

London, England
December 1814

Daniel Greaves, the Duke of Linwood, gulped down his final tumbler of scotch for the evening—or was it early morning?—as he stood from his seat on unsteady legs, the perfect vantage point to witness all the Christmastide festivities surrounding him. It was hard to determine if there was more bare flesh surrounding him or red-and-green-covered bodies, their flesh draped with holiday finery. His head swam slightly when he took the first step toward the door. Reaching out, he stabilized his balance and continued to the exit.

"Your coat, your grace?" a footman asked at his elbow, already holding out Daniel's overgarment. When Daniel made to take the jacket and drape it over his arm, the servant continued. "The temperature has plummeted since your arrival, and the wind is fierce. Allow me to assist you."

The gold-and-green-garbed servant held Daniel's jacket out, ready for him to slip his arms into the sleeves; as if he were a child needing an adult to keep him from falling ill for going out in the elements without proper attire. He wasn't a lad, hadn't been in too many years to count, but manners prevented him from saying as much to the footman.

"Leaving so soon, Danny Boy?" Phineas—Lord Gable—shouted across the room. "The morning is early yet, there's plenty of time to rush home for Christmas breakfast with your family."

There it was, confirmation the night had passed into the wee hours of Christmas morning.

"I really sh…ould be going." Dizziness coursed through Daniel when he turned to face his friend. "I need to be…" Daniel swallowed the bile that rose in his throat. "Going."

"Aw, well." Phineas inclined his head. "Give your family my best regards and wishes for the new year."

"Will do." Daniel slipped his arms into his waiting coat. Calling Phineas a *friend* was a stretch of their association. The man obviously didn't know Daniel well enough, nor *cared* to know him well enough, to know Daniel had no family. That he would return to his deserted townhouse to spend the holiday alone. Same as it had been since his father passed away seven years before. "Tell your family the same."

"Will do, Danny Boy."

Daniel cringed at the moniker. He'd hated it since the day Phineas had dubbed him with it at Cordell's, a gaming hell they'd both frequented several years before—the place they'd met. However, he'd never had the drive to *tell* the man he despised the name. That would signify Phineas meant something to him. The truth was, Daniel barely knew the man. They were not close, and they simply used one another for the same purpose: to keep away the loneliness and reinforce their miserable, self-serving lives. Nothing more significant lay outside their extravagant lifestyle of drinking, gambling, and women.

With swift fingers, certainly much more under control than they should be after the dozen tumblers of scotch he'd ingested, Daniel buttoned his coat. Female laughter filled the room when Phineas pulled a scantily clad woman onto his knee and tugged the front of her crimson gown down to reveal her heavy, rounded breasts.

It was something Daniel would commonly chuckle over, but the garish extravagance of the night had lost its appeal and he felt the draw to flee the scene.

Daniel flipped the collar of his jacket up and shoved his hands deep into his pockets as he pivoted and strode from the room, loud with drunken men and buxom women hoping to garner large amounts of coin when their night was done and their *services* no longer needed.

That it was Christmas mattered naught. Their nights were much the same, whether it be August or December.

"Your carriage will be brought round, your grace." Daniel nodded to the attentive butler posted in the foyer, noting that the servant didn't quite meet his eyes when he spoke. "You may want to wait here."

Another servant thinking Daniel needed someone to instruct him on what to do every moment. Was this how Phineas chose to live? Ordered about by compensated servants?

He clenched his teeth to suppress his irritation.

He was bloody tired—no, exhausted—and in need of his bed before the raging headache and hangover certain to follow his night of drinking arrived. "I will wait outside."

With a nod, the butler pulled the door open for him to depart.

Daniel did not pause to address the sympathetic look the servant bestowed on him.

The freezing early-morning air could only help clear his alcohol-addled mind and banish the pity he'd seen in the butler's stare.

Stepping out into the early morning, Daniel breathed in deeply, allowing the frigid air to reach his lungs—holding it there for longer than was normal—before exhaling. His breath swooshed from him, visible in the dark, yet several hours before the sun crested above the horizon to expel the intense chill.

"Good evening, your grace." The door closed on the butler's departing farewell.

A resounding, solid, final thud.

Daniel stepped off the stoop and into the open drive, no longer protected from the wind. A gust blew, chilling him to the bone, straight through his heavy woolen jacket. Maybe he should have listened and waited for his coachman in the warmth of the foyer. Though, Daniel already felt his mind clear, the breeze pushing the haze away much like the late-morning wind pushed the fog from the harbor. Daniel tilted his head back and closed his eyes. His head immediately swam, and he stumbled, but he refused to open his lids as he fought to regain his balance.

"You, there!" a man shouted.

Daniel sighed and turned toward the call. Who in the bloody hell was shouting for him? The twang of a coming headache pulsed behind his eyes.

"Stop!" Feet pounded against the hard-packed alley along Phineas's townhouse from the stables behind as a boy—no more than ten and two—came barreling around the corner, a livery servant close on his tail. "Thief! I said halt, before I sound the alarm!"

The child was almost upon Daniel where he stood in the shadows of the stoop, awaiting his carriage.

Quickly—far too swiftly for a man who'd drunk as much as Daniel—he reached out and snagged the boy's collar.

With a yelp, the child swung under Daniel's hold as his feet left the ground. It halted him, though he continued to pull and tug in protest.

"Let me go, ye tosser." The boy squirmed and kicked, trying to connect with Daniel's shin.

Daniel chuckled at the term, said in a voice several octaves too high for a lad.

"Thank you, your grace," the livery servant called. "My master has been called."

"Let me go, ye nob." The boy twisted to break free from Daniel's hold. "Me pa be look'n for me soon."

"What do you have there, son?" Daniel asked, sinking to a squat to have a look at what the boy attempted to hide under his arm. When the boy's feet touched the cobblestone, his wiggling nearly knocked Daniel to the ground as the child continued to struggle.

"I be no toff's son," the boy argued.

"All right, then," Daniel said. "What is your name?"

"I be Charlie, Charlie Drummond."

"Well, Charlie, what are you doing sneaking around Lord Gable's house at this hour?" Daniel asked. "You should be abed."

The boy snorted loudly; as if anyone with half a brain should know why he was about. "If I be sleep'n, then me mum and sisters be wake'n ta no food, ye toff."

"Then would it not be best to gather something to eat instead of loitering about Lord Gable's?" Daniel asked, staring pointedly at the boy.

Charlie removed the package tucked under his arm and held it out to show Daniel but did not loosen his hold on his treasure. "That's what I be do'n, ye blighter."

In his hands was a fresh loaf of bread wrapped in butcher paper.

"You stole this, young man?" Daniel stood, keeping a firm hold on Charlie's collar as he wrapped the bread once more and tucked it back under his arm.

"How else we ta eat?" Charlie spit out with a snort.

"That is a good question, son." Daniel rarely gave the lower class and their circumstances much thought. "Do you live close?"

"Let me go, ye toff," Charlie whined. "If'n the master catches me, he said he be make'n sure I never eat again."

Daniel chuckled at the boy's dramatic plea. "Oh, come now, Charlie. Lord Gable is an understanding man." And would never notice a loaf of bread had been pilfered from his pantry. Yet someone *had* noticed and given pursuit. Though Daniel couldn't imagine Phineas letting ol' Peggy off his lap long enough to handle the situation himself.

Following that thought, however, light streamed over Daniel's shoulder as the front door swung open behind him. The color drained from Charlie's face, and the bread dropped to the ground beside him, rolling free of its wrapping.

"Please, m'lord." Charlie's shoulders caved in, and Daniel swore the boy looked younger than before—frightened and helpless. "I be right—"

"What did I tell you the last time you were caught stealing from me?" Phineas's deep voice thundered behind Daniel.

Daniel turned to see a man he hardly recognized, Phineas's face flushed by his evening of being deep in his cups. Lord Gable had always appeared the blasé nobleman, unconcerned with anything that did not bring him pleasure. The anger that rolled off the man now was foreign and altogether unwarranted for such a minor offense as the boy pilfering bread to feed his family.

"I...well..." Charlie stammered.

"Gaines!" Phineas called to the livery who'd chased the boy around the townhouse. "Take the vermin to the stables. I will be round as soon as I make certain my guests are entertained."

Daniel winked at the boy and released his collar, but he stood frozen. "Now, Phineas," Daniel started, walking toward the man. "Charlie here is sorry, and he won't give you any more trouble." As if on cue, Daniel spotted his carriage coming round the house from the stables.

His host stepped off the stoop and strode toward Daniel, no visible signs of the massive amount of scotch he'd guzzled over the past several hours.

His eyes never wavered from Charlie.

"Your carriage has arrived, Linwood." Phineas jerked his head toward the approaching conveyance. "Have a pleasant Christmastide."

"I will see the boy home and speak with his pa about his thievery from your kitchen." Daniel set his hand on Charlie's shoulder and made to turn him toward his waiting coach, but the boy remained stock-still, staring at Phineas. "Come, Charlie."

"The boy will not be going with you, Daniel." Phineas shook his head, one auburn curl breaking free to land across his forehead, all informality leaving his tone. "This urchin and I have had dealings before. He's been caught stealing several times. I've warned him, and he continues to disobey me."

A chill ran down Daniel's spine when the man kept his eyes locked on Charlie.

It was a side of Phineas he'd never witnessed. His intense, focused glare was highly unsettling.

"You have guests awaiting you, Phineas." Daniel attempted to distract him once more. "Do not allow this to ruin your celebration. I can handle Charlie."

"That will not be needed." Phineas turned to his livery servant. "Gaines, bring the miscreant round to the stables. Now."

Daniel set his hand on the boy's shoulder. His thin frame quaked under the pressure as a gust of wind hit the boy in the face. A lone tear streaked down Charlie's face, leaving a trail of murky, dirt-streaked skin until the drop landed on the lapel of his thin, patched coat.

"You may go, Linwood." When Daniel made no move to depart, Phineas stalked his way, his boots thundering across the cobbled drive until he stood directly in front of him. Their noses were a mere inch apart. "Get in your carriage and leave."

Phineas's foul, alcohol-laced breath invaded Daniel's senses. If he hadn't already been deep in his cups, he would have become so from the fumes alone—not to mention the scent of cheap perfume made him woozy.

"I said go." Phineas lunged forward, shoving Daniel toward his carriage, putting himself between him and Charlie.

Daniel was uncertain what prompted him to regain his balance, take one last look at Charlie, and climb into his waiting coach; however, that was what he did.

Phineas was not a cruel man, not unreasonable. Certainly, he was not someone who would harm a mere child for attempting to steal a loaf of bread to feed his family on Christmastide morning.

Daniel would never injure a child, especially one who only sought to care for his family. Phineas was raised the same as he…a lord, with the proper decorum expected of men of a certain class and status.

"Where to, your grace?" his driver shouted once seated atop the enclosed carriage once more.

"Home." His command was barely out and the carriage in motion, pulling out of the curved drive, when the cries of the young boy reached him, following him until the early morning breeze was not strong enough to carry the sound any farther. "Turn around!"

Chapter Two

London, England
September 1815

A cannon blared in the near distance, followed by a command to charge, and the firing of muskets. It was so close, Lady Colette Hughes flinched, halting her neat stitching long enough to calm herself and steady her hand once more before plunging her needle into the broken, torn flesh of the soldier on the gurney. The thread pulled easily through the ripped skin, staunching the flow of blood from where the tip of a bayonet had been thrust into her patient's side during battle.

She pulled the thread taut and doubled back before leaning close to tie and bite off the end. There was no time to cut the string or for proper cleansing. Men would die long before infection set in if she did not complete her tasks efficiently and with swift, deft fingers.

The mud beneath her feet sucked at her worn boots as she stepped away from the table to allow another man to give the injured soldier a dose of laudanum to keep the pain from overtaking him.

She was uncertain when the rain from the storm had seeped into her workspace as the hours had melted into days of endless labor.

Acidic rust, the stench of fresh blood, filled the small medical tent she'd been assigned once the battle had begun two days prior. She'd argued men could not be properly treated when exposed to the harsh elements and the rain that pelted the area. Within the enclosure, the smell of rotting flesh, blood, and human waste was overpowering, yet Colette—Lady Lettie, as the soldiers called her—was determined to complete her task of aiding the wounded, regardless of the subpar conditions.

Lettie understood how fortunate she'd been to be chosen to journey with her husband's infantry regiment, and she would not let these men down. Six years of endless, mind-numbing travel, battles spanning several countries, and caring for wounds as insignificant as a dog bite to injuries as shocking as severed limbs and missing eyes.

War was not a kind master who rewarded the loyal with a future of happiness. It was a cruel bitch who stole a man's innocence and left him with nightmares he could not escape—even during his waking hours.

For the few women like Lettie, who'd dedicated and lost their own innocence to the hardships of battle and military service, the visions of wrecked bodies torn apart by cannon fire, musket shot, or rifle bullet did not ever go away. Alcohol to dim the hell of each waking hour was not an option for her. Many men—and their families back home in England—depended on her skill with a needle and thread, her steady hand when extracting shrapnel, and her knowledge of mixing powders to help with the brutal pain of the most severe injuries.

"Lady Lettie!" a man shouted, pulling back the flap on the tent. "M'lady. I brought him as quick as me feet could run."

Gus hurried into the tent, dropping the flap closed behind him and cutting off the sparse light from outside. A man was slung over his shoulder, not moving, and Lettie could see the blood soaking into Gus's coat. Clothing of any sort was as hard to come by as decent rations of food, and now Gus's only protection from the cold rain was ruined, the acidic, rusty odor would likely last just as long as the stain.

"Over here, Gus." Lettie waved the soldier to the only empty gurney remaining. "What injury should I prepare for?" She rushed to the small makeshift cabinet made from the discarded wood pieces of a broken-down wagon. Pulling the door wide, she inspected her ever dwindling stock of supplies. If the battle lasted much longer, she'd be useless to the wounded. Even her scraps of torn fabric for dressing wounds were almost gone.

"He be hit by a cannon and then pierced clean through by a fifer," Gus huffed.

Lettie heard the man swing the injured soldier onto the gurney as she collected all she'd need to treat the most severe wounds. The hurt soldier didn't so much as protest the jarring movement when his body hit the stiff board.

With as many supplies as she could carry, Lettie turned to her patient, muttering a quick prayer for the man. She trudged back through the muck, deepening by the hour from the continued onslaught of rain as it seeped into the tent. She sent another prayer of gratitude heavenward that at least she had a tent over her head and wasn't made to tend the wounded soaking wet.

She organized the bottles, poultices, and dressings on the small, tilting table beside her newest patient. "Gus, is he coherent?"

"No, m'lady." Gus removed his cap and clutched it before him, water streaming to the ground at his feet as his fingers gripped it, wringing out the rain. "Knocked senseless by the blast."

Lettie took in the prone form lying face down. "Can you roll him over so I can assess any injuries to his face and head?"

The man hesitated.

"We haven't all night, Gus," she huffed. "You know I cannot manhandle this soldier on my own."

The man sighed, his shoulders hunching, but he stepped forward and grasped the injured soldier by his midsection.

"Easy now," Lettie coached him. "We cannot risk harming him further. He has lost much blood."

As Gus carefully rolled the man over, another round of cannon fire erupted, and the ground shook beneath Lettie. Answering rifle shots filled the air, and the clank of swords and daggers rang on the breeze.

Gus's movement revealed a face she knew not only by sight but also by touch, smell, and even sound. She would know his shallow, leisurely breathing anywhere. Or the smell of the fresh scent he preferred. Even her fingers recognized the soft, even curve of his jaw and the dimple that showed when he laughed.

"Gregory?"

"I didna mean for ye to see him like this— "

"My love!" Lettie dropped the decanter of liquor she'd held in preparation of cleaning the soldier's open wounds—her husband's open wounds. The man was no longer a stranger. The bottle struck the ground and sank into the mud, not shattering. "Gregory! Can you hear me?"

But he remained still.

His chest didn't rise or fall.

His eyes remained open, staring directly at her, yet devoid of life.

"My lady." A rough hand shook her shoulder. "We are arriving at The George shortly."

Lettie's eyes fluttered open to find not Gus, but an elderly man who'd joined her in the coaching carriage in Dover. The rocking beneath her was not due to cannon fire but the moving conveyance. And no scent of decay or drying blood hung in the air.

"I did not mean to startle you," he continued.

She pushed up straight from her slouched position, her head tilted and leaned against the side of the carriage. She'd been lucky enough to gain a seat closest to the window. Her head pounded, and her neck ached from hours slumped awkwardly in sleep—a fitful, dark slumber that had given her no relief from the exhaustion she'd been unable to escape since that June day at Waterloo.

The single instant that had irrevocably changed every moment to come.

She'd awoken that day a married woman of over six years—and had ended it a war widow.

No husband, no home, no money, and no sense of future.

And only given a few days to reconcile all these facts before bidding farewell to Waterloo, packing her meager possessions, and setting off for England.

Lettie pulled her bonnet down to shield her watering eyes, though it was more intended to cover her short hair. In all the years since she'd shorn off her long, brown tresses, Lettie had never been embarrassed by her decision. Short hair was far easier to maintain and keep free of bugs while sleeping on the ground and traveling by foot. When she'd landed in Dover a few days prior, it had been with apprehension that she'd spent her remaining coin on a room with a decent bed to rest before her coach left two days later for London.

The other travelers had gone back to staring out the windows as they journeyed through the crowded, late-afternoon London streets, leaving her a spot of privacy to straighten her gown, button her overcoat, and secure her bonnet, ensuring that any wayward strands of unevenly cut hair were properly tucked. Her parents would likely not recognize her without her treasured tresses, famed as her only shining attribute. Long hair had always been one of the crowning glories of any proper English rose.

"Borough High Street stop!" a shout echoed in the crowded enclosed carriage. "The George. Only London stop."

Lettie watched as the five other passengers scrambled to collect their belongings and prepare for departure. There was no need for her to do the same. She'd traveled from Waterloo with only a simple sack of her most treasured possessions. Mementos, a portrait of her and Gregory on their wedding day, and an extra set of clothes. It was all she was able to carry on her back after leaving the battlefield and traveling across the Channel back to her homeland.

She'd left England the daughter of an earl—Lettie's mother a duchess in her own right—and returned a penniless widow.

The life she'd led before her marriage was of no significance to her. Lettie had never missed the finery and extravagance of town life. However, she *did* miss her husband. The hollowness in her chest grew ever more encompassing with each day that passed. Their love had been strong enough to endure years of hardships, traveling with the soldiers fighting Bonaparte. She'd come to terms with not starting her family and having children or the security of a home. She'd been willing to give all of that up to be with Gregory.

He'd been a brave, courageous man, dedicated to protecting all of Europe.

And now, she was left with no children, no place to call home, and without the man she'd promised to love and serve until her dying breath. She dashed away a rogue tear—she would not be reduced to a sobbing, weak female.

No one had told her *his* dying day would come before hers.

Every inch of her felt the loss of her soul mate.

Her heart barely beat, having lost the connection when *his* heart failed to beat.

Her fingers tingled restlessly, knowing they'd never again feel his warm skin against hers.

Her eyes no longer shone brightly at the thought of his return from a hard day's work.

Her legs scarcely moved, realizing they would never carry Lettie into Gregory's loving embrace again.

Lifting her gaze, she could only feel envy as she witnessed the couple nestled across from her, their hands clutched as they excitedly stared out the window, waiting for the carriage to stop. Pure jealousy spiked within her as the older man who'd shaken her awake caressed a small pearl brooch in his fingers…obviously belonging to someone he loved dearly and was likely to be reunited with soon.

It only served to remind her of how alone she was.

Soon, she would be reunited with her parents, yet she hadn't seen them in many years. They hadn't approved of Lettie's decision to marry a man without a farthing to his name and no title to speak of—despite her having told them that he could provide for her. And that was only what had happened six years prior. What about all she'd seen and been through since departing England? They could not understand the horrors of battle, the ungodly sight of a man lying prone with missing limbs, or the notion of holding a loved one as they passed on from this cruel world.

What if they never understood her?

What would she do then? With no money, no means of supporting herself, and no home to call hers, Lettie was at the mercy of others.

It was exactly as she and Gregory had lived their married life, but they'd found comfort in knowing they both believed in the war in which they fought. And when things became too overwhelming, they had one another.

Calls of greeting sounded outside as the carriage halted in The George's courtyard.

None of the good tidings and shouts of celebration were for her.

There was no way of knowing if her father had received her letter, informing him of her impending arrival. At best, her parents would be waiting to collect her. At worst, word had not reached them in time, and Lettie would need to find her own means of travel across London to her family's townhouse.

She'd done much more with far less.

Though she was remorseful over deciding to spend her remaining coin—collected for her by the surviving soldiers to make her way home—on a warm room and a decent bed. She hadn't even enough left over for a lukewarm bath to wash away the grime that had clung to her for more years than she cared to contemplate.

Waiting until everyone had disembarked the coach, Lettie stood and navigated the steps to the inn's courtyard. The driver held her simple tote out to her as her eyes fought to acclimate to the bright afternoon sun.

The yard was eerily quiet for the midday hour.

Lettie glanced around, hoping to see a familiar face among the disbanding people.

Maybe her parents had made better time on their journey than planned; however, the position of the sun as it descended toward the horizon told Lettie it was three o'clock.

There was even the possibility that they had received her letter and had chosen not to come and collect her. It was their right. After all, Lettie had gone against their wishes on more than one occasion.

Instead of making a spectacle of herself by dissolving into tears in the courtyard, she hefted her bag onto her shoulder and made her way into the inn's taproom to wait. No matter what their pasts held, her parents loved her. They'd often written to her over the years. Lettie was the only child of Lord Percival, and his wife, the Duchess of Essex, Lady Percival. As their only child, she was the heiress to her mother's Dukedom— even though her father's title and properties would be inherited by another male in the Percival line.

The dim interior of the taproom gave her a sense of ease that she hadn't felt in years. A few moments without being under the constant watch of others, whether in camp, on the ship to Dover, or the crowded traveling coach. Maybe the barkeep would take pity and offer her a drink, though she had no coin to pay for it.

If not, Lettie would wait for an hour or two, at most, before setting off on foot.

Glancing around the taproom, filling quickly with afternoon clients, she spotted a table nestled in a darkened corner, away from the door and foot traffic as patrons moved about. The table appeared clean, and the stools acceptable.

The smell of stale food and drink and hints of cigar smoke lingering in the air were far more welcome than the ever present smell of rot and rust on the battlefield. Why then did it cause her unease? Even at its worst—raw sewage clinging to the city streets—the odor of London should infuse her with a sense of hope, yet, on the battlefield, Lettie had known who she was. She'd been infused with an immense amount of purpose.

The familiar aroma of her hometown only highlighted her sense of being alone; no purpose driving her and less sense of who she was.

Lettie started across the room, keeping her head down as she hoped to discourage undue attention, but the smell of a savory, rich meal had her chin lifting and her mouth salivating with hunger. Several men gathered around a table close to the bar, plates overflowing with food, and tankards of ale before them.

It was a meal fit for a king—certainly not the widow of a fallen soldier.

"Barkeep!" the gravelly voice of a patron called, waving his hand to gain the notice of the man behind the bar. "When does the mail coach arrive?"

Lettie halted, turning toward the voice—a very familiar deep tone, though she hadn't heard it in many years. The rest of the conversation between the patron and barkeep was lost to her as she assessed the back of the man who'd spoken.

A group of men pushed by her and took the table she'd been heading toward.

No matter. She turned back to the gentleman at the bar. His back faced her, but his identity could not be hidden. Lettie knew the man too well, even after all these years.

A tendril of nostalgia coursed through her as the memories flooded her, pushing away her recent loss and filling her with a sense of youthful innocence.

Lettie longed to close her eyes and allow his voice to wash over her, a voice that had always been comforting...a feeling of home and security infused her.

Jet-black hair hung over the back of his collar. The length had been improper during her debut Season, and fashion had not likely changed since. His shoulders were tight, and his chin lifted with the arrogance of a man who knew his position all too well—so different from the young man she'd known, or thought she'd known. His tall frame sat heavily on the bar stool.

If he turned, would his midnight eyes—as black as his hair—be as bottomless as they'd been the final day she'd spoken with him, breaking the harsh news that she would marry another?

Lettie longed to run, depart The George before the man turned to find her staring.

But something deep within kept her rooted to the spot just inside the taproom, fearful that if she moved even an inch, her past misdeed would come crashing down upon her.

Chapter Three

Daniel swallowed the last of his ale before sliding his empty tankard away from him. The lukewarm, amber liquid traveled quickly down his throat and warmed his stomach—much like an old friend that one hadn't seen in many years. Damn, it felt good to have a bit of liquor in him after so many months of abstaining from drink. Every night after returning to his empty house, he wondered why he'd made the decision to refrain from alcohol, restrain his gambling, and dedicate less time to pleasures of the flesh. His friends had all but disappeared, little by little, when Daniel refused to participate in the merriment he'd enjoyed his entire life.

It only took a few moments of thought to remember why he'd been determined to cast aside his rakehell ways and become the man his father had raised him to be.

Blast it all but refraining from liquor brought back all the pain.

It was that hurt which enabled Daniel to focus on things more important than himself—and his pleasures.

Namely, his future. He'd even reconnected with his father's best friend, Lord Percival. It was why Daniel was sitting in The George's taproom, enjoying his first ale since that fretful morning at Lord Gable's townhouse.

He waved at the man again as he served another round of patrons, pointedly ignoring Daniel's question. "Barkeep. When does the mail coach arrive?" he asked more forcefully.

It was the only way he'd complete the task given to him by Percival. The earl had stated a package would be arriving at The George at three o'clock sharp and had said he would be eternally grateful if Daniel could collect it and bring it to Carrolton Hall. The townhouse was the Percival abode when the family was in London, which they had been more and more of late as the aging couple became less willing to make the journey to and from their country estate.

It was the least Daniel could do for the man who'd never turned him away, even after he convinced the earl calling off his betrothal to his daughter was a sound idea.

"Mail coach doesn't stop at The George, m'lord." The barkeep didn't pause as he wiped away a puddle of ale from the bartop and then stuffed his rag in his back pocket before removing several empty plates from a nearby table.

Daniel should have known things would not go as planned, they rarely did. "I am awaiting a package." Blast him for not inquiring further as to what the actual package contained.

"Stagecoach from Dover arrived not long ago," the man answered over his shoulder as he bent to clean another emptied table to prepare it for new customers. "Think it is still in the courtyard. You can check with Straton, the driver, to see if he brought anything other than passengers."

With a gruff, "Thank you," Daniel stood from his stool and stretched. He'd arrived far earlier than needed and had been perched on the tiny seat for far too long. His back was tense, and his legs were cramped, and the time had given his mind more than ample opportunity to dwell on things better left bottled up and stuffed deep inside, forgotten.

The taproom had filled with patrons at some point—Daniel hadn't noticed—and it was necessary to weave his way through the crowd toward the door, sidestepping several travelers too weary to move to allow him to pass. Daniel kept his stare on the light filtering in through the open door. The stench of dirt and grime drifted off every person as he finally made his way out into the courtyard, and to a breath not filled with stale ale or human stench—as fresh and unmarred as the air could be in London with hordes of people crowding into every available space anyway. Nevertheless, the air, untainted by stale liquor and the smell of unwashed bodies, happily filled his lungs.

The driver, Straton, leaned against the empty coach, scribbling in a logbook.

"Sir." Daniel stepped before the man. "Do you, by chance, have a package for Lord Percival?"

"I not be carry'n anythin' but people, m'lord." Straton didn't so much as glance up from his writing. "People and luggage be all I carry. No room for nothin' else."

"Are you certain?" Daniel made to look at the log in Straton's hands. "Mayhap you can check your paperwork."

"Are ye deaf? I not be transport'n anythin' but people and their baggage." He snapped the logbook shut and trained a cold stare on Daniel. "Now, if'n ye don't mind, I only have an hour's time afore I be off again. I need ta find meself a hot meal an' a pint."

Percival had sent Daniel on a fool's errand, a waste of his time. However, Daniel had naught else to do. The earl could have as easily sent a servant to collect the package and not requested Daniel handle the matter personally.

The coach driver—and the barkeep—were mistaken, or Lord Percival was losing his senses. Something Daniel didn't want to contemplate. He had much yet to learn from the older man.

His fist tightened and then released. Rushing to conclusions would help no one, especially Daniel.

Daniel pivoted toward the inn to locate someone who could give him answers or direct him to the nearest mail coach stop. The last several months working with Lord Percival had filled a part of him that had been empty for many years. It had given him purpose, and a reason to wake up each day for something other than finding a high-stakes gaming hell and a bottle of scotch. It was almost like having his father back. He'd spent much time with both men in his youth, as his father and the earl had been close friends, sharing everything from hunting trips to holiday celebrations. And, in turn, Daniel and the earl's daughter had spent years gallivanting about their country estates and exploring the gardens of their townhomes.

He was uncertain what had brought the woman to mind as she'd been away from London many years.

The crowd from the stagecoach had settled, with anyone who hadn't departed the inn courtyard immediately was seated and enjoying a meal or a tankard of ale. A barmaid assisted the man behind the counter, carrying plates to and fro.

Daniel spotted the driver in a dimly lit corner of the room, his face lowered as he continued to scrutinize and write in his log.

He'd gained the same answer from the barkeep earlier, so Daniel turned, continuing into the foyer of the inn in search of someone with useful information.

An elderly woman, her sleeves rolled to her elbows, and her greying hair tied back in a severe knot, stood behind the counter, a welcoming smile of greeting on her face. "Good day, sir. I am the proprietor's wife. Do you need a room?"

"No." Daniel returned her smile, pushing a lock of black hair behind his ear. "I was sent to collect a package coming from Dover. However, the barkeep informed me The George is not expecting the mail coach, only the stagecoach today, and the driver told me he only had passengers and luggage."

"That is true," she confirmed. "The mail coach does not stop here. I am sorry you were misinformed."

"That is not your fault, ma'am." Daniel nodded in thanks. "One last question. Does the mail coach stop anywhere near here?"

The woman tapped her finger against her chin in thought. "We drop our mail off at a building about fifteen minutes' walk north of here, past the market." She grabbed a paper and a nub, hurriedly noting an address. "Here. The footman in the courtyard can get you headed in the right direction."

Daniel took the paper she held out to him. "Thank you again." He inspected the address while the woman hurried back to her duties. The name and direction of a solicitor's office greeted him. Percival was not the type to confuse something as simple as the location of a delivery, though Daniel need remember that the man was aging by the day. Even more so since seeing his only daughter off to war when she'd decided to follow her new husband. A prickle of sorrow bubbled up. Daniel was quick to press it back down where it belonged. It only gave way to the betrayal he'd thought he conqueror long ago, rising and sparking his anger and disappointment with a woman he'd thought he knew— until she left with little more than a half-hearted explanation. No, he would not think of the past...especially her.

"I believe the package you were sent to collect is I, Daniel."

He froze, afraid to turn and dispel the hope that suddenly overtook him and extinguished his anger. It was as if a pail of icy water had been dumped over his head. It could not be her. Percival would have told him if she'd returned to England. His lungs burned, begging for air to relieve the strain from his frantically beating heart.

If he turned and was not greeted by the angelic, heart-shaped face framed by brown curls and featuring intense, deep blue eyes, he'd perish on the spot. Despite his heartache and unease, he wanted nothing as much as he wanted to turn and see *her* standing behind him. How many times had he thought he'd spotted her across a crowded ballroom, or traveling in a passing carriage down Bond Street, or promenading in Hyde Park?

He'd lost count of the number of times he'd pushed his way through a flock of people or turned his horse about and given chase on his way to the racetrack—but every time had resulted in the same end. A startled woman, and Daniel appearing the lunatic on his way to Bedlam.

Not today—in this crowded inn. He would not appear the man lacking in senses and cause a spectacle of himself.

Daniel had aged since Lettie had fled England, that fate was not reserved solely for her father. As the years passed, his longing for her—for the connection and bond they were supposed to have—erased the old him, only adding to his sense of loneliness.

Slowly, he turned…certain that disappointment once again awaited him.

Chapter Four

Lettie pulled at her bonnet, attempting to hide her shorn locks from his view and then tugged at her coat, a size too small for her. It had been so long since she'd felt even a prickling of doubt with regards to her appearance. On the battlefield, no one gave her a second glance as long as she tended to the wounded, kept the cooking fire blazing, and mended uniforms.

Unthinkable that the mere presence of a man from her past would have Lettie acting the insecure debutante of her misguided youth. *Not misguided, never misguided*, she chastised herself.

There was nothing more she could do about her haphazard appearance. She was a soldier's wife—*was* being the operative word. Now, she was nothing more than a soldier's widow. She'd experienced things far worse than a crowded taproom at The George and faced harrowing circumstances far greater than the scrutiny of these strangers.

She would not be ashamed of her appearance; yet still, embarrassment heated her cheeks.

Even standing here before a man she'd once thought she would spend her life with, she should not hide herself in shame.

Lettie straightened her shoulders. Confronting the man she'd jilted did not frighten her. She had no regrets about her choice to marry Gregory and follow him into battle. In fact, at the tender age of twenty, it had been the only thing she'd been certain of.

The man before her was a drunkard, a scoundrel, and a gambler—or he had been when she left.

Daniel Greaves, Lord Linwood, her childhood friend and confidante, turned with agonizing slowness.

When his glare settled on her, she noted the stiff line of his jaw and the tense set of his shoulders. Lettie didn't remember him being so...hardened. He'd been untroubled and lighthearted in their youth, only concerned with things that affected him. He'd spent each day in search of pleasure and fun, ignoring his duties and her.

But now, something had changed.

Then again, she had changed, too.

Though, he was as handsome as she remembered. His ebony hair was so dark in the dim lighting it almost appeared blue. His skin was tanned, much like hers, but that could be a trick from the limited glow of the room.

His boyish appearance, however, was gone, replaced by an older version of his former self—empty and lifeless. His hooded glare finally softened as he settled his gaze on her face.

Betrayal lanced through her, sizzling down her spine. She was in mourning for her late husband—whom she loved and adored. Thinking any man, even one she had all but wed, was handsome was an offense and disparaging to Gregory's memory.

"Colette? It cannot be." He took a step toward her before halting, his stare surveying the room. "Are you alone?"

It was obvious her father hadn't told Daniel of her return, or explained why he'd undertaken the task of collecting her—he didn't know it was her he'd been sent to collect. She had also noted her parents never mentioned Daniel in their frequent letters. She'd often asked after him, but they'd always sidestepped those sections of her writings, refusing to write even a simple word of him.

"It is I, your grace." She suspected he'd chosen another bride, married and started a family of his own. Lettie knew once her and Gregory's service was over, they'd return to England and settle at her mother's country home—an estate and title that would settle on her one day, or so the letters patent had established decades before—and she'd be forced to see Daniel again, a wife and children at his side. "I am alone but for my traveling…sack." She shifted her shoulder, repositioning the bag she carried.

"Allow me to carry that." He took the final step toward her and took hold of the shoulder strap, attempting to alleviate the weight. Unfortunately, her bonnet strings had become wound in the strap of her tote, and when he hefted the bag onto his shoulder, the covering fell from her head, revealing her short hair. He cleared his throat and turned toward the door before continuing, "My carriage is waiting outside. It was wise of me to bring it as opposed to my horse."

A pang of hurt smacked her when he continued to avert his stare from her noticeably lacking locks. She reached up and pushed one short curl behind her ear.

"Yes, I suppose the long walk to my parents' townhouse would be uncomfortable in Hessians," she replied, hoping a bit of levity would bring his eyes back to hers. It had been so long since she'd been free to gaze into their inky black depths. However, they remained averted, as they had since she'd snatched back her bonnet. "But I assure you, I am quite an able horsewoman."

She nodded to the barkeep and followed Daniel toward the door. At some point, clouds had covered the bright afternoon sun, and a light drizzle had begun.

He paused, and Lettie almost collided with his back. "I guess the London weather is another reason I brought the enclosed coach. This way." With one final shrug, he lifted her bag and dashed out into the rain, moving swiftly toward his carriage, the growing puddles never slowing him down.

There was no other option but to follow and pray she didn't slip along the way. She greatly needed a bath, but falling in a dirty mud puddle would do nothing to help her.

Lettie grasped her skirt in both hands and bounded out of the inn, circumventing a puddle. The sensation to giggle rose in her throat, but she clamped her lips shut. No matter how unexpected this moment, chasing after an old friend in the rain, was, she was still a woman in deep mourning. No one around her knew, but she did, and laughter of any kind was not acceptable, especially since her heart continued to bleed. If she laughed—if the cavity holding in all her despair, sorrow, and anguish were pierced—everything would come spilling out. She wasn't ready for that. Not with Daniel so close. Truly, not with *anyone* close.

She'd been fixated on the source of her suffering since departing Waterloo. It was the only way she knew how to keep her grief from exploding outward and her mind from wandering so far she lost track of time and place. If that were to happen, Lettie would not be able to collect the pieces of herself to move on.

No, any cracks in the hard shell she'd constructed around her heart would mean a fall into utter helpless despondency.

Gregory would not want that for her.

He'd lived in the moment; gone wherever he was needed. He had fought—and died—for a cause greater than both of them combined.

He deserved better than her laughter.

She didn't deserve to be happy or find any amount of joy while Gregory lay in that meadow, unable to experience another moment.

She owed him fidelity…and better than her laughter at a hurried run through the rain. Gregory would never again feel the cool, fresh raindrops upon his face.

Lettie stopped at Daniel's side as his coachman opened the door, holding the sack Daniel had given him.

"I will take that." She grasped the tote from the servant and climbed into the carriage unassisted, settling on the rear-facing seat. With trembling hands, she tucked the sack next to her on the cloth bench and turned her attention to her lap.

She could not allow her meager possessions to be stored in the carriage boot. What if there were a leak and the rain ruined her only portrait of the man she loved?

Would always love.

Lettie could not bear that. No, she'd had a difficult enough time keeping her belongings safe during her travels. She would keep them close until she reached the shelter of her home.

Not *her* home, her parents' home.

The only home she'd known over the last six years was a bedroll beside Gregory—or the medical tent she was afforded when the soldiers were not moving.

The carriage shifted and creaked when Daniel entered, taking the bench across from her. She'd forgotten how tall he was and how his shoulders seemed to take up the entire width of the conveyance.

From his unease, she sensed he had many questions. Lettie didn't have to take her gaze off her lap to notice. The continual tapping toe of his Hessian said it all. When he experienced anxiousness or uncertainty of any type, he fidgeted. A tapping of a toe. The clicking of his teeth. A nervous tug on his cravat.

Everything had changed in the last six years, yet…nothing at all.

She still knew him well.

Lettie risked a glance at him from under her lowered lashes, but her stare moved no farther than his hands sitting lightly atop his knees. The knuckles of one hand were bruised, and his skin appeared rough, similar to that of a workingman. A farmer, millworker, or soldier.

Her own hands were too filthy, stained by years of hard labor, to note if they were worn and rough, as well. Dirt clung to her fingers—still trembling from the shock of seeing Daniel after all these years—and settled beneath her fingernails, short from nervous biting.

The simple gold band on her finger—given to her on the day she'd wed—sat heavy on her hand, though it held no adornments of filigree or gems.

She twisted the ring on her finger. It was the only thing of monetary value she possessed, and it would not gain her enough to secure lodging for longer than a fortnight. Not that she ever planned to remove it.

"Will Mr. Hughes be joining you in London, Lady Lettie?"

Her glare snapped to his and Lettie couldn't stop her eyes from widening, allowing him to see her despair. However, the sorrow he witnessed could never compare to the complete heartbreak within her.

Chapter Five

It had been a simple question. One Daniel thought would be expected given Lettie was a married woman. A way to begin a conversation after so many years apart—after so many years of living different lives. The slump of her shoulders and the shaking of her hands as she twisted her wedding band on her finger told a far different tale.

"Lettie," he began quietly. She appeared the timid mouse, something his childhood friend—and once betrothed—would have never allowed. "Look at me, please. I did not mean to upset you. It was only a question."

When her eyes met his, they were as round as his mother's ancient tea saucers and held as much wear. But at twenty-six, no woman's stare should hold so much…hurt.

Its depth reached across the carriage and tangled about his own heart, pushing him away from her.

Daniel reclined on the velvet-covered bench, stretching his legs out and crossing them at his ankles.

Next, he turned and looked out the rain-splattered windowpane as the carriage sped away from The George. Suddenly, he wished he'd have succumbed to another tankard of ale.

His calm pose appeared to do nothing to banish the tension from her; did not still her worrying fingers that'd moved from her gold band to the stitching of her coat—a garment that was at least two sizes too small for her. The sleeves didn't reach her wrists, and the elbows were almost threadbare.

Maybe beginning with a question was a bit too much for her.

Daniel shifted on his seat and pretended to stare out the window once more. "Your mother will not take kindly to your choice of hairstyle, my lady."

He thought of sharing that he thought the style framed her face perfectly and highlighted her deep blue eyes, or mentioning it showed off her graceful neck to perfection, but an unladylike snort filled the carriage, bringing Daniel's gaze back to her.

Lettie narrowed her stare, honing in on him, and he immediately regretted his comment. He was zero for two in the way of tries.

He was mucking up the conversation and making a fool of himself.

"Long locks are not preferred among women who travel with the soldiers. Hair collects bugs, and those bugs spread to rations. Not to mention they itch like the devil when one tries to sleep." She paused, and Daniel sensed she'd learned that lesson the hard way. It was his turn to stare at her wide-eyed. "Bathing is rare in times of battle, and a proper head of long hair needs constant maintenance and brushing. With so many wounded, it

46

was hard to find the time and adequate supplies. I much prefer this *style*, as it is."

A lump formed in his throat, and he coughed in hopes that it would vanish, but it remained, giving Lettie the opportunity to sharpen her tongue on him again.

"When one is faced with carrying extra soap or laudanum for pain management, there truly is no choice to be made," she continued, the words leaving her in a rush as if she'd finally found an agreeable topic that suited her. Her chin notched up and she stared down her nose at him. "Hair is only a vain attempt to shield others from who a person truly is. I have dispelled with all the fine draping society deems necessary for a woman of worth. My hair is not who I *am*, though it may be who I *was*."

Her eyes lost their piercing glare as if she'd been transported to another time by her own words.

If Daniel had found it difficult to speak before, it was near impossible now. She'd always been idealistic, and he'd blamed it on her flight-of-fancy ways—always determined to think the best of others, to give as much as she could to the less fortunate. Like giving a new coat to one cold fruit vendor at the playhouse would solve the many societal problems London faced.

The *beau monde* may be able to look past her long locks to admire the stunning woman behind them; however, he was certain they would never be able to notice beyond the lack of hair.

It was a sad revelation, but the wretched injustice of it would not diminish just because it was deemed so.

"My apologies for the discourteous observation."

"There is no apology necessary, Lord Linwood." She crossed her arms, mimicking his pose. She'd never called him by his title—not in direct address. They'd been acquainted long before he'd inherited it, and when his father passed away, it had always still been *Daniel*, as she was simply *Lettie*. "I have steeled myself for such uneducated and insensitive remarks, I assure you."

The young, impressionable woman who'd left him—and England—was no more.

The angry, hurt, and lost lady before him was unfamiliar.

A stranger.

Lettie was gone. Even Lady Colette, as she was properly addressed, had disappeared.

Before him sat a woman he didn't know. Yet, he desired to know her...*had* to know her, at least enough to vanquish the sorrow from her eyes.

But how was he to do that if every time he spoke, his words were met with anguish and fury?

"Lettie," he whispered to the woman before him, only familiar in appearance. "What happened to you?" He poured every speck of concern he had into those words as he trained a tender stare on her. Something awful had happened, something had changed her—and he wasn't sure it was for the better.

"Gregory is dead." She brought her hands to cover her mouth as if surprised she'd spoken.

"Dead, Lettie?" He shook his head to do away with his confusion. "I am so deeply sorry for your loss."

It was then Daniel realized the change from optimism and light was not a hardening of her, but rather a spiral into despair and sadness. Her dark garb should have alerted him to her reason for returning to London.

"Thank you for your sympathy, your grace," she sighed, the tension leaving her shoulders as her posture turned inward. "But there is so much more than the loss of Gregory. There are men dying every day during battle, and not only from wounds obtained during combat, but also from disease, famine, and…heartbreak. Women and children are left without their husbands and fathers. At least I was fortunate enough to travel with the man I loved for six years. There are many who will never know the fate of their loved one."

She tugged her bonnet from her head and ran her fingers through her shorn locks, massaging the back of her neck.

Knowing the fate of a loved one who never returns from war is far different than knowing and having to deal with the loss. Avoiding a known truth is harder than remaining blissfully unaware.

Lettie may be conflicted about how to come to terms with everything, but Daniel was utterly baffled. She seemed to find more compassion for those lost during battle, but neglected to fully explore and heal from the loss of her husband.

"Why did your parents not send a carriage for you?"

"I was unable to send word of my homecoming until we reached port in Dover," she confessed. "I used what little coin Gregory and I had managed to save over the years—and the few funds given to me by the other soldiers—to purchase my seat on the stagecoach. My funds did not allow to me find lodging for an extended period of time."

"I am happy you arrived safely, and I am certain your parents will be, as well." Even after all these years—all the hurt he'd suffered when she'd begged him to break their betrothal agreement so she could wed Gregory and depart with the soldier—he was happy to have her near again. "Your journey must have been harrowing. A hot bath and a warm meal surely await you at Carrolton Hall." He glanced out the window. "It is not far now."

No matter what Daniel had seen in the past year—the things he should have stopped—it was nothing compared to the horrors Lettie was burdened by. Carnage and death impacted a person.

Daniel had seen enough of death, and he fully understood the weight it left on a person's shoulders. He could not fathom the extreme strain of bearing witness to hundreds—or even thousands—of such atrocities.

Chapter Six

Lettie stood frozen in the vestibule of Carrolton Hall, a place that should be familiar to her. She'd spent every London Season in this home when her family was in town. She'd run the halls at all hours of the day and night, helped Cook prepare meals in the kitchens, bottle-fed a litter of kittens when their mother had been hit by a carriage, and even hosted a gathering in her mother's salon in hopes of gaining funds to help the homeless children who found refuge on London's streets.

She'd hidden in her father's study and devoured novels full of adventure. She'd dressed for her debut ball in her mother's chambers. She'd kissed Daniel for the first time in the butler's pantry. And she'd called off their betrothal in her parents' dining room.

However, in that moment, as she stood there a changed woman, the grand home could have been Africa—though not a painting or rug had been moved since she'd last been here.

Nothing had changed. Not the décor in the foyer, not the scrutinizing glare from her parents, and not Daniel at her side.

She still did not understand why he'd allowed her to end their betrothal.

She'd never asked. Hadn't remained in England long enough to inquire what he'd gained from the situation.

Lettie's eyes strayed to Daniel, infusing a speck of resolve within her at his confidence.

Pushing her treacherous thoughts away, Lettie managed a weak smile for her parents, Barclay and Julianna Downing, Lord Percival, and his wife, the Duchess of Essex. They were as stately and matched as they'd always been. However, her father's golden hair was now shot through with grey, and the duchess had taken to applying white powder to her blotchy skin. They'd aged. Remorse coursed through Lettie at the part she'd played in it all.

"Mother, Father." She curtseyed to each in turn. "It is lovely to see you both."

Silence stretched before Daniel cleared his throat and stepped forward, giving the earl and duchess a proper bow. "I am certain you have much to discuss, and many years to catch up on. I will leave you all and bid you farewell."

"Yes, many thanks, Linwood, for retrieving my daughter." Her father nodded in dismissal.

Next, Daniel turned to her, his eyes searching hers. Lettie suspected if she begged him to stay, he would; however, her parents had already asked much of him. "Thank you for seeing me safely…*home*, your grace." The word stuck in her throat. This did not feel like home. The bedroll she'd shared with Gregory held more warmth than her parents' townhouse.

"Lady Colette." Daniel set her sack down on the polished floor beside her and took her hand. "Do send word if you are in need of anything."

He placed a quick kiss on the back of her bare hand, released her, and turned to depart.

Mercifully, the front door shut behind him before he could glance over his shoulder to see the flush that'd spread to her cheeks as she watched him go. Over the years, Lettie had given up on wearing gloves or so much as keeping a suitable pair within her meager wardrobe. There was little hope she'd be able to hide it from her parents.

"My dear Lettie." The duchess closed the gap between them and wrapped her only child in a tight embrace, though the stiffness of her arms and the tension in her back did not go unnoticed by Lettie. The earl and his wife had never been overly affectionate with her, or one another. "We are pleased to have you home. Though it is very unfortunate Gregory is lost to us."

"He is not lost, mother," Lettie mumbled into her mother's hair. "I laid him to rest in a meadow not far from camp. I could not afford the coin to have his body brought across the Channel."

"Ah, well," Lord Percival's ever-rational tone cut in. "It was likely for the best. I can only imagine the stench."

When she gasped, her mother removed her arms and hopped back in alarm as her father's face blanched, realizing the horrid implication of his words.

"My apologies, Colette." He stepped forward and gave her a quick hug. His embrace was not as awkward at the duchess's, but still little better than hugging a stranger. "And my condolences on Gregory's passing."

"Thank you, Father." Lettie hefted her sack to her shoulder.

"Allow Darling to take your things, my dear." The duchess had no more said the words than their butler was at Lettie's elbow to take her possessions. At her hesitation, the duchess continued, "He will make sure they are placed in your room."

Lettie allowed her grip on the strap to loosen and handed the bag to the servant. "Thank you, Darling."

"It is lovely to have you back, Lady Lettie," he responded with a beaming smile. "The servants are bursting at the seams to greet you."

"That will wait until she is properly bathed, fed, and gowned," her mother scolded.

Lettie noted her mother's list did not include rest. Sleep was what Lettie needed most. She only hoped her bed offered the comfort the rest of her homecoming lacked.

"Tell the servants I am greatly looking forward to seeing them all." Lettie couldn't help but return Darling's smile. "Let Cook know I have gained an entirely new appreciation for her skills in the kitchen after so many years cooking every meal in a single pot."

"Of course, my lady." Though the man's voice was cheerful, his eyes gave her a compassionate glance before he hurried upstairs with her sack.

The duchess slipped her arm through her daughter's and steered her toward the receiving room. Lettie didn't react at the way her mother's nose wrinkled when she moved close.

Lettie almost laughed, knowing her mother wanted nothing more than to flee from her daughter's side and seek her own bath to wash away any stench that may have transferred from Lettie's unwashed body to her own. Instead, Julianna Downing, always the poised duchess, lifted her chin and escorted her daughter into her finely adorned room, her father trailing several paces behind them, as if not willing to risk having the smell embedded in his own attire.

"Come, please sit," her mother chimed in her ever-present polite manner. She'd been raised to serve as the Duchess of Essex—much as Lettie had been groomed to do the same—and her manners never faltered. "I see Eldora has already delivered tea for us. Sit, sit, sit. We have much to speak of."

When her mother waved her to the chaise across from her own favored seat, Lettie respectfully sank to sit, crossing her legs at the ankles and tucking them below her. It was very rare, indeed, that Lettie had been afforded a proper chair; however, her upbringing and decorum were still ingrained in her every move.

"Thank you for allowing me to stay with you," Lettie said as her mother prepared three cups of tea. Her father preferring more cream to actual tea, while her mother took hers without accoutrement. Lettie's was a perfect blending of the two: tea with a small helping of cream.

"My heavens," her mother sighed, handing Lettie her steaming cup. "Where else would you go?"

She'd pondered the same question as she'd sailed across the Channel before dispelling any notion of reaching out to Gregory's family for shelter. Her husband had been the third son of a viscount and only afforded what his family saw fit to give him or what he'd earned as a soldier—which nearly hadn't been enough to see Lettie home. Her parents were her only option unless she decided to find work as a governess or seamstress until she inherited her mother's Duchy.

And it seemed her parents knew that fact as well as she.

"Lord knows Gregory left you with very little." Her mother's exaggerated eye roll was enough to tell Lettie they may have forgiven her for marrying beneath her, but they had not pardoned Gregory for capturing her heart and leaving her a penniless, homeless widow. "And that family of his…they do not deserve you."

A pang of remorse shot through her—Lettie had never properly introduced her parents to Gregory's family. Truthfully, after the wedding, she and Gregory hadn't remained in town long enough for Lettie to know them either.

Lord and Lady Stanhope were not unkind people. They had provided for her and Gregory for the few days after they were wed and before they departed to join the soldiers in the Peninsular War. In fact, they'd more than happily assisted Gregory with gaining his commission, though if they'd written after she and Gregory left England, her husband had never shared their letters with her.

"Now, Julianna, do not speak ill of poor Gregory's parents," the earl chimed in, though his flat tone indicated his lack of conviction in his own mutterings. "What your mother meant to say, dear, is that we are happy you are home—where you belong—and we know society will welcome you back with open arms. Linwood already has, I dare say."

And there was the core of the matter: pleasing society and finding a new husband.

"I have no plans to enter society before my year of mourning has expired," Lettie confided, but did not speak of her true intent to never join the *ton* again.

"Oh, that is preposterous!" Her mother's teacup and saucer rattled at her outburst. "Gregory was a virtual unknown. I dare say three months is a more than appropriate mourning period. I have taken the liberty of scheduling an appointment with the modiste."

Three months? That meant her mother expected her to shed her dark garb within a week's time. "I will not. It is too soon…" Words failed Lettie.

"Do you think Lord Linwood will wait around for another nine months to renew your betrothal?" Lord Percival muttered.

Lettie turned to her father, an accusing stare making him shrink back. "You expect Daniel and I to resume our plans to wed? After everything that happened and all these years?"

She'd thought Daniel would be happily wed by now with a graceful, proper wife and a growing horde of children. He was an eligible, handsome lord with a wealthy estate. All things that attracted marriage-minded matrons.

"Certainly." Her mother wisely set her teacup on the table, and Lettie followed suit. "He is unwed, and you are in need of a husband, one who will manage your birthright, my Duchy."

"We trust the estate to no one but Linwood," the earl confirmed. "He knows the land, our business affairs, and will treat you as you deserve."

Lettie had lost the man she'd thought to spend her life with not three months prior, and they expected her to forget him, forget the years they'd spent together and the horrors she'd seen, to marry Daniel and take her place in society. Take her place as the Duchess of Linwood—that was until her mother perished and she became one of the few women in England to hold a double Duchy. The Duchess of Essex by birth and the Duchess of Linwood by marriage.

"You wish for me to put the last six years behind me and plan for my future immediately?"

A reassuring smile lit her mother's face and the woman nodded. "I knew you would understand, my dear."

"No, actually, I do not understand," Lettie fumed. Her fists balled in her lap. If she'd been holding the delicate teacup, it would have shattered in her grip. "I have spent many years traveling with the British troops across more miles than I can count. I've witnessed death firsthand—my own husband died right before me—and, without further thought, you want me to forget all that and prepare to enter society for a second time?"

"Well…now that you put it that way…" her father stammered. "It…well…I can see—"

"Do not back away now, Barclay," the duchess scolded. "This is exactly what we agreed would be best for Colette when she arrived home. She thought herself in love with her husband, which one cannot think to have twice in one lifetime. Settling for a match borne of friendship is far more than is to be expected for a widow—even one of such high worth."

"We never agreed to discuss it when she first arrived," her father retorted. "We were to let her get settled into her room, see her old gowns, and let entering into society be her decision."

Which meant they'd planned to dupe her into believing it was her idea to move forward, to put her unsavory past behind her.

Lettie glanced between her parents. The earl outright avoided her glare, while her mother scrutinized her without remorse.

The mere thought of leaping back into society terrified her, yet there was little she could do to dissuade her mother once she'd set her mind to something. There was one thing that would convince the duchess to allow her daughter a few more months to grieve the loss of her husband.

Lettie reached up and untied the string holding her bonnet in place and pulled it from her head. Her chin tilted up a notch, matching her mother's.

"Colette!" her father squawked at the same time her mother yelped and fell limp in her seat. "Julianna, my love!"

The earl stared between his wife, unconscious in her seat, and his daughter, her famous tresses shorn almost to her skull. He was stunned into indecision as his wife slipped from her chair to the floor before he snapped into action and hurried to the bell cord to summon help.

Lettie stood and inched toward the door when a servant rushed into the room. The thump when her mother hit the floor must have alerted the household, as a woman in Essex colors of scarlet and gold came into the room, smelling salts at the ready.

Her father leaned over his fallen wife, whose eyes fluttered as she regained her senses after the servant waved the vial of smelling salts below her nose.

It was one of her mother's most practiced techniques of gaining exactly what she sought.

Unfortunately, Lettie had witnessed a man truly faint from the shock of a musket ball colliding with his shoulder. She'd seen another soldier pale and crumple to the ground when he realized a bayonet had ripped into his leg. She knew firsthand that when a body fell to the ground unconscious, it was soundless—a fact she should share with her mother at some point.

Lettie breathed a sigh of relief as she slipped out the door and started toward her room.

Chapter Seven

Daniel adjusted in his stiff-backed chair, attempting to keep from eyeing the knot on the Duchess of Essex's forehead. It was turning an odd shade of purple with hints of blue. He'd never been called a particularly observant man; however, he was certain the lump had not been there when he'd arrived earlier with Lettie in tow.

Clearing his throat, he glanced around the dining room to see servants lining the walls, prepared to serve dinner.

He'd expected the evening to be a bit awkward, but this was downright uncomfortable. His first instinct had been to send his regrets when the invitation had arrived to join Lettie and her family for dinner. But again, as always happened where Lettie was concerned, he'd pushed aside his unease, knowing she could use him at her side.

"I do not know what is taking the girl so long," the duchess huffed. "It is not as if she has hair to style or dozens of gowns to choose from. She even turned away her lady's maid, said she was more than capable of dressing herself. Can you imagine, Barclay?"

Lord Percival appeared to also choose to ignore his wife's blemished forehead. The earl instead smoothed his cravat and straightened his utensils on the table in front of him before turning to Daniel.

"Lord Linwood, my wife and I thank you for collecting Colette from The George today." He glanced over Daniel's shoulder toward the door as if hoping that mentioning his daughter's name would cause her to magically appear. At least then, it would not be her father's responsibility to keep the conversation from veering too far from what was proper. "We are overjoyed to have her returned to us. Though the circumstances are not ideal, as I am certain she told you."

Daniel knew exactly what information the earl was attempting to extricate from him, and part of him wanted the man to continue wondering if Lettie had opened up and shared her devastating news. "Yes, very unfortunate Lady Lettie has been through so much heartache."

"If she had only done as she was raised to do, none of this would have occurred." The duchess's matter of fact tone left no room for argument, though Daniel could find many things wrong with her statement.

Namely, Daniel wasn't certain he would have been able to wed a woman who was in love with another. Nor would he have doomed Lettie to a future with him when she desired someone else. Even if he hadn't been overwhelmed by his father's passing and taking over the Linwood title, he still would have allowed her out of their betrothal agreement.

It had been the honorable thing to do—for everyone concerned. That fact had not changed.

Though he could not honestly admit he'd done it at the time for *honorable* purposes.

"Good evening, Father." Lettie quietly closed the door behind her, and Daniel prayed she hadn't heard the conversation at hand only a moment before. "Mother. Lord Linwood. My apologies for my tardiness."

"Do not worry, my girl," Percival said as he stood to welcome her. "You are here, that is all which matters."

She allowed her father's embrace but her back remained rigid, and she appeared uncomfortable with the action.

"Do sit." Her mother nodded to the open seat beside her, and a servant stepped forward to pull back her chair.

Lettie stepped slowly around the table, giving Daniel the opportunity to take in the sight of her. She'd bathed and styled her hair in a tiny pearl clip; however, lines of exhaustion still etched her face. The dark grey gown she'd selected hung on her lithe frame. Odd, because Lettie had never been considered ample in size, but now, she was far thinner than he remembered.

"Why in heavens have you chosen that dreadful rag?" The duchess's irritation over Lettie's gown choice was obvious. "No matter. A trip to the modiste will solve all your problems, and you will feel much improved. I will contact her immediately to schedule a fitting for you."

It would take more than a visit to a Bond Street modiste to even begin to help Lettie through everything she'd experienced in the past several years.

Her scrunched brow and pinched mouth confirmed she believed the same.

When Lord Percival and Lettie took their seats, the earl motioned for the meal to be served. Servants entered the room, one after another in an endless display, as plate after plate and pot after pot were set upon the long table in a grand display fit for a king. The only way the many platters of food would be consumed was if all the Essex servants joined them at the table and filled plates; however, after the lids had been removed, the servants fled the room, leaving only four footmen to serve.

Succulent duck soup, pheasant with plum sauce, three types of bread, and pieces of cheese were heaped upon each of their plates.

"Father," Lettie sighed. "This is far too much."

"Nothing is too much for my daughter's homecoming meal, I assure you."

"No, I mean this is far too extravagant. There is more food on my plate than a soldier is rationed for an entire week." Lettie turned an exasperated glare on her father. "This is wasteful."

"What has gotten into you, child?" her mother huffed. "Show your father the respect he deserves. It is not his fault he provides well for his family and those he loves." She turned a grimace on Daniel as if to apologize for Lettie's outlandish behavior.

Daniel had been wrong to accept the earl's invitation to dine with them on Lettie's first night in London. It was evident they needed more time privately, as a family, to reconnect and familiarize themselves with one another once again.

Yet, he'd needed to see Lettie again, be close to her if only to soften her discomfort of returning to England.

"Mother, I do hope you instructed your maid to apply ice to your forehead." Lettie took her utensil in hand, and he and the earl breathed a sigh of relief at the same time. "The bruising will last a week or so, but the swelling will recede sooner if you ice it several times a day."

He was taken aback by her knowledge. She'd spoken of her chores as a soldier's wife, though he'd envisioned her preparing meals and mending clothes.

"Yes, your maid instructed mine; however, Darcy confirmed that nary a mark remains." The duchess lifted her chin a notch and turned her attention to her plate as silence fell. Only the sounds of a servant filling Lady Lettie's wine goblet could be heard as the table at large focused on the meal.

He watched as she expertly wielded her knife, cutting her pheasant into tiny morsels and spearing them before taking her first bite. When her eyes closed and her head tilted slightly back, Daniel could almost hear her moan of pleasure at the tasty bite.

The duchess glanced at her daughter as she too took a forkful of the fowl before setting her utensil aside. "It will be nice to have you at my side once more, Colette."

"Please, Mother, it is Lettie," she said, narrowing her stare on her plate. "No one has called me Colette in many years."

"Be that as it may, my friends—all of society, truly—know you as Lady Colette." When Lettie's glare snapped to her mother's, the woman acquiesced. "But, of course, if you prefer Lady Lettie then I will not argue over the matter further."

"That is kind of you." Lettie lowered her spoon into her soup, but did not bring a taste to her mouth. "Lord Linwood, it is nice of you to dine with us. I would expect you to have other pressing matters to attend to this evening," she said dryly.

Daniel had waited for her to mention something along those lines, and he could not blame her for her snide comment. "Actually, there is no other place I have to be this evening. Although, I do appreciate your concern with my daunting schedule," he replied with an eyebrow raised.

She was quick to quarrel—as if she remained on the battlefield, disregarding his attempt to be her ally, not her foe.

But he'd taken her bait so quickly. He needs must remember she was grieving, and people handled their grief in many different ways. He'd thrown caution to the wind and taken to his rakehell ways after his parents passed away. Who was he to judge her prickly manners?

"I am sure there is a gaming hell or tavern that is missing you…and your funds," she said, not taking her glare from her soup bowl.

He would not allow her remark to spark his temper. "Actually, I find I have lost interest in gambling and drinking."

"Is that so?" Her brow rose in question.

"It is." His utensils scraped against his plate as he cut into his meal.

"Linwood has been working with me, learning to better manage his estate and take his place in parliament," Percival interjected. "Been very happy to have him, I have."

Daniel chuckled. "Happy to have him" was an understatement. The elder lord treated him as the son-in-law he had been meant to be, going so far as to show Daniel the ledgers from the duchess's many estates, which would eventually belong to Lettie.

Lettie stuffed another forkful of food into her mouth and chewed slowly, keeping her eyes downcast.

It brought to mind their final meal as a betrothed couple before she'd announced her plans to marry Hughes and follow him to war—with or without her parents' approval. Daniel had arrived to escort Lettie to a ball, already deep in his cups with the sweet scent of his ladybird upon his coat. He'd tripped over the threshold of her townhouse and virtually tossed his coat and hat upon the foyer floor when he'd learned she was still dining with her parents.

Daniel had marched right into their dining room and sat across from Lettie.

He'd been a scoundrel. Never an attentive suitor.

He'd been young and still reeling from the loss of his parents.

She'd been the only constant thing in his life, the only person who grounded him. The one person who put up with his deplorable demeanor.

That night, she'd had enough of him and ended their betrothal. And, like the fool he was, he'd agreed to let her go. Actually convinced himself it would serve him best not to be tied down to any woman permanently. Contracts, gossip, and scandal be damned.

She'd already met and thought herself in love with Hughes at that point.

Lettie had looked exactly as she did now.

Sullen and a bit green. Though then, he hadn't realized she'd been wracked with nerves over breaking their betrothal, knowing it would cast a bad light on them both, as well as their families. He'd already lost his entire family. She was all he had left to lose.

He'd wished for years after that evening that he'd have been clearheaded enough to notice her anxious turmoil. He could have put her mind at ease without bringing around her abrupt confession of love—for another man.

"Lady Lettie," Daniel said, watching her closely. "Are you feeling unwell?"

She stood so quickly, the servant behind her was unable to pull her chair back to allow her departure. The tiny bauble she'd pinned in her hair skidded across the floor. The high-backed chair tilted so far back, Daniel thought it in jeopardy for falling completely over and knocking clear through the wall.

"Lettie, do stop with the hysterics!" the duchess screeched.

Daniel also stood, pushing his chair back with less force to follow as Lettie fled the room.

"I will tell you, Barclay, that girl is not fit to take over the Duchy," her mother whined. "Whatever are we to do?"

"She will adjust," Daniel called over his shoulder before departing the dining hall after Lettie; though her parents were not making anything easier for her.

"Six months, my dear," Percival answered. "We shall give her half a year. Then I will step in and set her straight. The chit must select a proper husband or take her place among the aging widows."

Daniel wished he hadn't heard those final words. He could not picture Lettie wedding another man.

Chapter Eight

Lettie wrapped her arms tightly around her midsection as she ran down the hallway. She sped up and turned a corner, then turned yet again when the corridor split in two directions—losing track of her location within the house. The hem of her shapeless gown caught on her slipper, and Lettie tumbled forward before catching herself and righting her balance.

The hall opened into the large kitchen area, Cook and the other staff busy tending the garden beyond the window.

Her stomach rolled, and waves of nausea brought her to a halt.

The aroma of a cooling pie on the open window ledge only served to cause her midsection to cramp further as she doubled over in pain.

She hadn't eaten much, but what she had managed before her stomach revolted had been delicious. Far more savory and flavorful than any meal she'd had since departing London with Gregory. There had been nights when her hunger had been so overwhelming she'd dreamt of Cook's pastries, mutton stew, and fresh, roasted vegetables grown in their garden.

Those memories—no matter how pleasant—belonged to a different time, a different Lettie. The woman who could enjoy an afternoon covered in flour and helping bake pies was gone. She'd learned quickly the cruelty waiting in the world outside her gilded cage.

Why, oh why, had she prodded Daniel about their past? He'd been nothing but a gentleman since collecting her at The George, and she'd repaid him with spiteful comments. If he hadn't been willing to allow her to break their betrothal, her life would have been very different today. It was her parents she was furious with—at least in part—as well as Gregory for getting himself killed and leaving her.

It was possible Lettie would have never learned the harsh realities of the world, never experienced loss, and most certainly would have continued with her fanciful ways and grand ideas for helping others.

In recent years, she'd seen the big picture, gained a deeper understanding of the actualities of life. Feeding one hungry man did not solve anything. Making certain one child had a home was not enough for her. She'd witnessed mass casualties in the Peninsular War and at Waterloo. She'd seen utter devastation firsthand, the same hands that had worked tirelessly on wounded and injured soldiers. Her palms had been coated in blood countless times, and she'd seen other women left with nothing when their men fell on the battlefield.

Her parents and much of society knew nothing of the destruction war caused.

They knew nothing about losing a loved one in such a violent, tragic, senseless way.

They knew nothing of the mental willpower it took to get up each day, knowing you'd see more of the same until you worked in a mechanical state from sunup to sundown, your entire body becoming numb to everything, and your mind so scattered it was hard to concentrate on anything else.

And her mother could speak of nothing but frilly gowns and society engagements.

"Lettie?" Daniel called from the doorway.

Her stomach settled at the sound of his concern, and she turned to face him. "I apologize for my abrupt departure. My years away from London have jeopardized my societal decorum."

Why did her nerves settle whenever he was near? It made little sense to feel peace around Daniel.

Yes, they'd been close. Yes, they'd been slated to marry their entire lives. Yes, she'd once cherished his friendship. However, he'd changed once their betrothal had become official. He'd turned to debauchery instead of chivalry. As a suitor, he'd been lacking in many ways. He'd suddenly preferred drinking and carousing with other young lords than escorting Lettie to the theater or spending time in the library. In those final months, Daniel had all but pushed her into Gregory's arms, albeit unknowingly. It was because Daniel hadn't shown to escort her to an afternoon musicale recital that Lettie had met Gregory in the first place. It was one of several planned outings her betrothed hadn't bothered to show up for.

She turned away and gazed out the window to where the kitchen servants worked in the garden, in an effort to hide the tear that streaked down her face at the thought of Gregory. They'd never again sit side by side and listen to off-key debutantes sing or share a meal of sparse rations and stale bread.

With one last sigh, she forced her misery down and steeled her back before turning. A smile or even a weak grin was still too much for her.

Daniel jerkily pulled a hand through his tussled hair.

"Thank you for your concern, your grace, but I think I am only fatigued and in need—"

"Stop with the bloody tales, Lettie." He strode to her, grasping each of her arms just above her elbows. "And I am not Lord Linwood, or 'your grace,' it is Daniel. We have known each other since birth. Bloody bollocks, we kissed. Once, long ago. I am not a stranger. I am not some man who knows nothing of you or the hurt you suffer from. I understand grief well, Lettie. What plagues you is far more than exhaustion."

"How could you—a titled lord with nary a thought to those losing their lives at war—know anything about what I have experienced?" Her harsh words drove him back a step. "While you were safe and well-fed, I was on the front lines. I was tending the wounded. I was starving. I was cold most nights."

"There is naught I can say but sorry for all you've faced."

She straightened her shoulders and notched her chin. "And I will tell you again, there are no apologies needed. If I had the option to relive the last six years, I would do it again—without thought or hesitation." Though, she'd be wiser now and not as shocked by the disappearance of her innocence.

"And that is the Lettie I know. A tenacious, strong-willed hellion. A force of nature." His eyes danced as he

73

took in her attire. "Though, I must agree with your mother, even a war widow should dress in finer garb than an old dust rag."

Everything about him was genuine, from his encouraging grin to the easy set of his shoulders. Could she trust him?

It was an odd thought to have. They'd known one another their entire lives, but how could she trust a man known for his love of liquor, women, and gambling? He'd willingly given her up, not so much as a single word to convince her to change her mind. Not that Lettie would have believed him or stayed in England. Her mind had been made up by that point.

He'd chosen everything above her: liquor, gambling, and debauchery. He'd put those trivial things above her, and she'd allowed it. She'd run away and done something with her life while he'd continued to drink himself to death.

"And you are wrong." He turned and sat on a stool close to the counter, gesturing for her to take the other open seat. He turned and folded his arms on the island top, not waiting for her to decide to sit or remain standing. "You may not believe this, but before you married Gregory, you were the only person I had. My father had passed the year prior, and I was still grieving. In his honor—and at your father's insistence—I solidified our courtship. But I was hurting."

Lettie had never thought about how her marriage to Gregory had wounded Daniel. He'd always been the lighthearted sort, going with the current of things, and doing what others did or what gave him optimal pleasure.

"While a father dying, and a betrothed marrying another, are not the same as a husband passing away in battle, I can understand your need to grieve."

"He died right before me..." Lettie was uncertain why she felt compelled to offer up the information. Daniel's stare never left his clenched hands in front of him. "You know my parents expect you to renew our courtship and announce our betrothal in short order."

"I have gotten the impression, though they have not said as much." He turned to face her, bringing her legs to settle between his. Each on their own stool but their knees touching. It was more connection than Lettie had experienced in many months, and her heartbeat increased at the closeness. "But I do know I will never allow you to be coaxed into a situation you are not comfortable with. I did not demand you wed me six years ago, and I will not demand it in the next six...or ever if that is your wish."

His words soothed her. At the same time, they raised several other questions—none she was ready to ask. "They say a marriage borne of friendship is better than living my remaining years as an aging widow. But I have known great love. How is it possible to enter into another courtship?" Especially since she'd known love, and now knew the lack of such deep emotion would hang like a cloud over every moment.

Daniel reached forward and wrapped his solid arms around her, pulling them both from their stools to stand.

Heat pooled deep within her, in a place that had only stirred when Gregory was near.

Lettie concentrated on the feel of Daniel's large hands as they stroked her back, but that only ignited the spark into a full-fledged flame in the sensitive spot between her thighs.

For the first time in many months, she felt safe and protected.

She *was* safe and protected in Daniel's embrace.

He would never allow any harm to come to her, of that she was convinced.

But with that knowledge came the realization it had been far longer since she'd felt secure. Had it been years? Possibly since she'd wed Gregory and departed England for battle. Certainly, Gregory had loved her, but had he protected her from harm?

The only thing she knew for certain was that finding any pleasure from Daniel's embrace was a betrayal to the man she claimed to love.

Chapter Nine

Every inch of *him* was acutely aware of every inch of *her*. Lettie's soft curves to his hard, unforgiving hulk. They should not fit so well together. He should not be holding her now, smelling the scent of vanilla soap on her short hair and dreaming of never letting her go.

All the while, he suspected she thought of another man. Wished to be embraced by *him*, not Daniel. Longed to smell Gregory's scent rather than the sandalwood Daniel favored.

Why was he so willing to take any little bit of closeness she offered? Even this intimacy, knowing it was another she desired. Besides, Daniel wasn't in need of solace; it was Lettie who'd experienced a harsh blow. He should be giving her comfort, but instead, he couldn't think past the idea of tilting her chin up to accept his kiss.

Too soon, she pulled from his embrace, or was it Daniel whose arms fell to his sides first?

"I am sorry, I did not mean—" Lettie started, retreating behind her stool. "It is, well, I have been so lost since Gregory died."

He held up his hand to stop her words. She'd thought of Gregory when embracing him, that much he'd known, but he could not handle her saying it aloud.

He'd spent years thinking of her, imagining her; so much that he did not want to be faced with the reality that she hadn't been doing the same.

Her eyes narrowed once more when he resumed his seat on the stool. "You have learned all about me. Now, what has happened to you since my departure? You seem oddly…*changed.*"

The shift in topic pleased him—anything to banish thoughts of her dead husband, though speaking of himself had never been pleasurable for Daniel. Maybe with Lettie, it would be. They'd kept so much from one another in their youth: her falling in love with another, and his devastation over losing his parents. He'd pushed her so far away, he hadn't even noticed that losing her had sent him completely over the edge and into utter debauchery. It had been either find solace in booze, gaming, and brothels, or cry himself into oblivion, alone.

But how much to share with Lettie? Never would he want her to feel responsible for the life he'd chosen.

"I am older and settled into my place as a duke. When called 'Linwood,' I no longer feel the need to search for my father," he said, not admitting that it had only been the past several months that he'd taken his position seriously. He could never tell her how far he'd fallen in his rakehell ways. Never would he admit that the day she'd married Gregory, he'd found comfort in a bottle of scotch and the willing arms of several strumpets. "After you left, and with both my parents gone, I needed time to adjust."

"And you have, from what my father has said." Lettie relented and sat back down but made no move to face him directly. "I do not expect you to forgive me for running off with Gregory, but I loved him very much." She paused, taking a deep breath. "Still love him with every ounce of feeling left within me."

"There is no need to explain," he replied. "I told you then as I said today, I will never pressure you into anything, whether that me a betrothal or sampling a bite of snail."

She laughed, but it held no depth.

"Yes, I very much appreciate that, though I wanted you to know that what Gregory and I shared, no matter how brief our marriage lasted, was real. Deep. A love like that only comes once in a lifetime."

A love he could have shared with Lettie, except he'd been a fool. He'd allowed distance between them, bottled his emotional state, and caused her to run into the arms of another man. A man who'd been more than willing to give her the love and attention she deserved. A love that Daniel hadn't been capable of then.

"I plan to hold that love close, for it must last the rest of my days." She placed her hand on her heart, and her eyes drifted shut for a brief moment. Daniel wondered who she saw when she did, but her next words made it all clear. "It was you who allowed me to experience true love and passion. And for that, I will always be grateful."

Lettie only saw Gregory. A war hero.

A man who'd been brave enough to not only claim Lettie as his wife but also give up his life for others on a battlefield.

Daniel held no hope of ever comparing to him.

He hadn't even been man enough to step forward and save that street urchin from Lord Gable's cruel hands. He glanced to the pies cooling in the open window, the kitchen servants working beyond in the garden, and guilt flooded him once more.

Lord and Lady Percival had been wrong to set their sights on Daniel as a match for their daughter. She was too noble, too generous, and far too pure for him.

He was a scoundrel, a rakehell, and a debauched man.

Had been.

The thought swirled around his musings.

But, in Daniel's experience, a man was who he was. Ultimate change was impossible.

He'd given up on himself and any future he could have shared with Lettie. That she'd returned a widow did not change anything.

And that thought only brought him to his feet with a hasty farewell and a whispered, "Good evening."

A bottle of scotch and a loud, distracting crowd called to him as he bolted from Carrolton Hall. If she called for him as he fled, Daniel didn't hear her.

Chapter Ten

Lettie's horrified stare darted across the battlefield. The dead, dying, and wounded lie clustered in groups or decidedly alone. One man leaned against a stout tree, pinned in place by the broken point of a bayonet. The soldier, a man she'd met on occasion during meals—Oliver. His eyes were open in terror, yet she knew he saw no more. The tilt of his head pointed the opposite way as if to say that what she sought would be found in that direction.

He was wrong. Lettie didn't want to find anything. She wanted to run, desired to put miles and oceans between her and the war that'd been her life for so long she didn't remember what peace felt like. The battles that kept her and Gregory moving, traveling across foreign lands, and never worrying about a family or home of their own.

Lifting her skirts, Lettie knelt beside a fallen soldier—a French soldier, but that meant naught to her—and felt for a pulse at his neck.

Cries for help came from every direction. There was no way their encampment had enough supplies to treat even a fraction of the fallen men littering the blood-soaked ground and strewn in every direction.

Unfortunately, the French soldier had no discernible heartbeat. His vacant stare should have confirmed as much without her wasting time feeling about his cold, lifeless body.

Lettie stood, noting that at least one of the puddles of crimson hadn't soaked into the rough ground below her or been washed away by the ever-constant drizzle, for the hem of her gown had absorbed it and the stain now wound its way into the cotton fabric of her skirts, inching higher by the second. It was her only stipend gown, in blue and red. It would likely be weeks before she could procure a new bolt of fabric to make a fresh one.

Lettie didn't dare glance above the hem to see the rust-colored smears staining the material at her knees from when she'd knelt before the man.

Something brushed against her leg, and Lettie flinched, pivoting to see what offensive thing lay close. A mound of discarded bodies lay at her side. Where had they come from? She could have sworn that they hadn't been there when she'd knelt next to the fallen French soldier. The pile rose and fell as if it were a living, breathing entity.

"Colette." The moan of her name drifted on the tainted breeze.

Who could be calling her? No one called her Colette—it was "Lady Lettie" or "Doc" unless she was cooking or darning clothes, then it was "Cook" or the unfortunate, "wench."

Her glare darted around the field, searching for whoever had called her. They must know her. Perhaps from London or her family's country estate.

"Colette!" The moan was louder this time. "Lady Lettie."

The ground shook beneath her, and she realized that the pile of bodies called to her.

Whoever it was, lay right beside her. She could find them, help them, save them!

She dropped beside the tangle of limbs, clothing, and forgotten weaponry, but was uncertain where to begin or how to disentangle the mass of moaning, wounded cries.

Lettie reached out and rolled a body from the top of the pile. It continued to roll until she heard a thud as it settled in a large, muddy puddle. She worked furiously, her arms ached at the dead weight, but she'd yet to find the man who called to her for help.

He must be close. He still said her name, but it was louder now—growing with intensity as she worked faster.

The ground trembled once more as if a cannon had been shot right beside her, but no other sound filled the air other than her ragged breathing and the shout of her name.

Blessedly, she pulled a limp arm away to reveal a familiar face. His mouth formed her name one last time.

Just as quickly, all life drained from his eyes.

Lettie was too late. She hadn't moved fast enough. She hadn't known the true urgency of the matter.

Daniel!

"Daniel!" the single word ripped from her, breaking the silence as Lettie's eyes snapped open. Above her, Daniel stood—mercifully alive—staring at her with great worry, his hands holding her shoulders firmly against the lounge. "Daniel," she sighed, allowing the terror to drain from her, and her body to go limp, no longer fighting his hold. "I must have fallen asleep."

He released her and took a step back, permitting her to sit. She pressed her hands to her coiffure to make sure her pose hadn't ruined her maid's handiwork, but belatedly, she remembered her locks were shorn too close to her scalp to afford any style beyond an unassuming clip.

She breathed deeply, attempting to slow her erratic heartbeat enough to stop the trembling of her hands before Daniel noticed.

"You were calling out in your sleep." He took a seat next to her on the chaise. "I came to meet with your father, but I heard you yelling all the way in the foyer. You sounded as if you were in great pain, and the servants were acting as if they did not hear anything amiss."

Great pain was not a strong enough phrase to encapsulate the hellish night terrors she'd suffered since Waterloo. Only this time, something had changed. The wounded, dead, and dying were as they were every night when the dreams came. The eerie quiet—except for the moaning of the wounded—was as it always was. Even her name reaching her on the breeze, calling her forth, deeper and deeper into the blood-soaked battlefield— and farther from camp—was the same.

However, the mound of breathing bodies had been larger.

As she'd moved the final limb to discover who'd been calling to her for help, it had not been Gregory's cold, unmoving eyes staring at her, but those of…

Daniel.

He stood quickly and moved to the sideboard, pouring her a healthy goblet of watered wine before returning to her side. "Here, have a drink. You are as pale as a freshly laundered bed sheet."

Before taking the offered glass, Lettie ran her damp hands down her legs to her knees. The added time would hopefully stop their shaking and enable her to hold the wine without spilling it on both of them.

"Thank you," she said with a feeble smile. It had been nearly a week since she'd spoken with Daniel. He'd come and gone from Carrolton House but he'd never pressured her to accept his presence as she adjusted to being back in London and under her parent's care. Oddly enough, a part of her longed to see him, speak with him, and be close to someone who knew her well. "It was only a dream, nothing more. I am much better now."

"How long have the nightmares plagued you?" he asked.

His matter of fact tone told Lettie that lying would do her no good. Yet she wondered what Daniel had lived through to know anything about the nightmares that visited her during sleep.

# # #

Her brow furrowed. "How do you know it was a nightmare?"

"You were thrashing around." He lifted his arms where a red welt had formed. "Your fist knocked me before I was able to get a handle on you. If you were dreaming of kittens and rainbows, you would not have been so..." He paused to find the exact word to describe the scene he'd walked in on. "...out of control and filled with terror."

She stared into her cup, and Daniel regretted inquiring about her fitful sleep. Since that early morning at Phineas's townhouse, the same terrors had infiltrated his once peaceful slumber. Endless hours spent running and searching the stables, trying to locate the boy as Daniel heard the whip hitting him repeatedly, over and over, while Charlie wept for his mother.

Daniel was never able to stop the beating, only locating Phineas by his deep chuckles of pleasure when they echoed through the stables. And each morning, Daniel had awoken feeling like the failure he'd proven himself to be.

Every night, it was the same.

It was his penance.

He deserved the nightmares that visited him every time he closed his eyes.

But Lettie…Lettie deserved none of it.

And she certainly deserved a better man than Daniel had proven himself to be.

"What are you doing here?" she asked, her voice still gravelly from her fitful rest. "Besides meeting with Father, that is."

She'd always known when he was keeping something from her. It was a blessing that she hadn't honed in on his much bigger secret. "I thought I'd accompany you to the modiste, instead of the duchess. I overheard your mother informing the earl that your appointment was scheduled for this afternoon. I would much enjoy escorting you."

Her brow rose. "Why?"

"Well, I know how taxing your mother can be, especially when she has her sights set on something," he said. And Daniel had desperately missed Lettie. He'd gone so far as to make several unnecessary visits to Carrolton Hall over the last week in hopes of gaining a glimpse of her or hearing her voice float down the long corridors. "I offered to escort you, which will give you the freedom to select material and styles you prefer as opposed to those forced upon you."

She appeared to think over his offer, and Daniel feared she'd decline his escort.

"However, I should probably inform you that the offer has already been made and accepted by the duchess." He winked.

"I suppose I should thank you." She stood, the color having returned to her face. She glanced over her shoulder at the tall clock against the wall. "I will collect my cloak and meet you at your carriage."

As she hurried from the room, the need to pull her close and into a hug filled him. He shook his head to clear the silly notion. She was only retrieving a warm coat, not running off to battle again. In no time, she'd be in his carriage, and they'd be off and away from the prying eyes of her mother.

If he were lucky, Lettie wouldn't cross paths with her father. Or she'd find out Daniel hadn't a meeting with the earl at all but had overheard her mother mention a fitting with the modiste at sharply eleven o'clock today on one of his needless social calls disguised as a meeting. It just so happened that he hadn't any previous engagements to call off in favor of an afternoon with her.

Though, he would have canceled a meeting with the King himself to gain an afternoon in Lettie's company.

After their embrace on the night of her return, he'd gone home and stared at his decanter of scotch. He couldn't bring himself to take so much as a sip of the fiery liquid, nor had he sought out a gaming hell or brothel. For the first time in a long time, he knew the consequences of his actions and realized that either choice would result in him hurting Lettie again, even if she never found out.

He'd told her he would never push her into accepting a marriage proposal from him.

And he'd meant every word, even though his promise to his parents nagged at him daily.

Daniel's respect for Lettie meant more. He would not disappoint her again. Returning to his drunken, rambunctious ways would most certainly disappoint her. And with that in mind, he'd promised himself to give her space and time to adjust to town life—gain her own footing without his constant presence.

Accompanying her to the modiste and offering to be her friend did not make up for all the wrongs in his past, but it was a start.

When he exited the front door of Carrolton Hall, Lettie was already seated in his open-air carriage, her poise returned and a bonnet covering her brown locks. It must be the doing of the duchess because Lettie had never been fond of headgear; but then again, many things had changed in the last six years. Gone was the pile of curls that had always been pinned high atop her crown, and in their place, was a style much more suited to combat life.

"Are you ready, my lady?" He took his seat across from her as she fussed with the string of her handbag. At her nod, Daniel called to his coachman to be off.

They had a bit of a distance to travel, especially with the midday traffic as society made their way about the city on social calls, shopping, and trips to Hyde or Regent's Park, especially since he had one stop to make before arriving at the seamstress's shop.

Silence stretched between them.

Daniel watched Lettie.

Lettie kept her stare trained on anything but him, yet not noticing that their carriage did not head for the modiste shop as planned.

While she appeared relaxed and calm now, her mouth had been contorted in a silent scream while she'd slept—before she'd called *his* name…not her late husband's name, but Daniel's. She fought her demons during her sleep, and he'd been there with her. But in what form?

Had he saved her?

Had he been the cause of her pain?

Daniel didn't know, nor had she been willing to speak of it more in the salon.

At the moment, they were stuck in a carriage, alone, in the middle of slow-moving coaches and men on horseback, affording them ample space and time for a private conversation.

"How often do the nightmares come, Lettie?"

"Every time I close my eyes, even when I'm not asleep," she confessed but did not look at him.

He hadn't imagined they plagued her so often. Even his night terrors were absent every few nights when he went so long without rest that he fell into a slumber deeper than death.

"When awake, I can sometimes keep them at bay, but I have no control over my sleeping mind." She turned, and he noticed the dark circles under her eyes.

Why hadn't her fatigue been as evident when he'd collected her from The George?

"And they started after Gregory passed?" Daniel didn't want to mention the man's name, did not want the ghost of her dead husband invading their private moment; however, it was Gregory's fault that Lettie suffered so. If he'd never met her, never made her fall in love with him, never married her and whisked her away to war-torn areas, she would not be plagued with horrible dreams now. She would not be pining away for a man who was long buried.

And maybe, Daniel would have found his own happiness and not fallen into disgrace.

Thankfully, his carriage turned onto St. James and continued down the street barely wide enough for two carriages to pass. It was then that Lettie stiffened, finally noticing that they'd turned off the main street leading toward the popular Bond Street shopping area and onto the street that housed the Linwood family townhouse—his home.

"Where are we going?" she feigned ignorance, but her eyes immediately looked down the street and settled on the brick façade of Daniel's house.

"I thought you'd relish a few moments in a familiar spot—one without the ever present watchfulness of the duchess." Daniel fell silent as this coachman did exactly as he'd bid, turning onto the narrow lane that would lead to the alley bordering the back of the Linwood property were a small grove of plum trees blocked the view from outsiders, including the Linwood servants. "I know it is highly improper, but I thought we could spend a bit of time here before your meeting with the modiste."

He stopped himself from reminding Lettie of the solace she'd found in his family gardens when her mother's ranting became too much to bear; however, the softening of her stare told him he'd made the correct decision.

"You always found peace here," Daniel muttered, keeping a close watch on her, prepared to command his coachman to drive on if their destination did not please her.

"And silence…" She spoke barely above a whisper, and if he hadn't been paying such close attention to her, Daniel would have missed her words. "It was the silence I loved most."

"You are welcome to come any time it suits you." The carriage came to a stop at the stone wall separating his property from the common alley. Odd, but he came here for the complete opposite reasons as Lettie. She came for peace and solitude, while Daniel came in hopes of finding Lettie and a few brief moments of witty conversation, jests, and tree climbing. They'd laughed, they'd played, and they'd enjoyed time as a young woman and man—not a future duke and duchess with unlimited responsibilities and the welfare of others hanging about their necks, weighing them down. "That is if you desire it."

She turned, and a pained expression settled on her face, before she gave him a small smile. "It is very kind of you, Daniel, to remember." Her mouth moved to a frown. "But I find the quiet is not to my liking anymore."

"Then we shall climb trees and swing from one branch to the next, like we used to when we were children." Daniel flung the carriage door wide and departed, holding his hand for her to take. "Come, Lettie, let us climb to the highest branch and yelp as loud as we dare!"

She shook her head but her grin returned, with only a hint of the melancholy she'd shrouded herself in before. "I do not think it proper to climb trees nor scream, but I would very much enjoy a walk in the grove."

Taking his hand, she stepped down from the carriage. Daniel tucked her hand into the crook of his arm before setting off for the wooden gate that led to the back of his property, shielded from view of the house by the ancient plum trees.

"Agreed, no climbing and no shouting." He made an X over his chest as they walked through the unlocked gate and into the overgrown foliage of their long ago special spot. "What about a game of chase the weasel?"

She let out a light laugh at the memories of the game they'd concocted during their childhood. "You know well and good that I was always faster than you."

"Yes, but I fear those heavy skirts weigh far more than the ankle-length frocks you wore as a child." He raised his brow at her in challenge. "There is no conceivable way you could best me now."

"Mayhap I have no need to best you." Her smile fled once more, and Daniel sensed her slipping away from him again. He was uncertain where her mind traveled to, but he'd noted this occurring her first day in London. There was nothing Daniel longed for more than to keep her here, solidly with him and not in the past. "Tell me, Daniel, what have you been doing since I departed London?"

Imbibing too much. Thinking too little.

And making an utter mess of his life as he applied himself to filling his days with people, activities, and things that hadn't mattered.

Until that fateful Christmastide morning, that is.

But Daniel would not share any of that ugliness with her. Lettie had seen enough, experienced far more than a gently bred woman should in her short lifetime. He would speak of the last nine months. A time he was proud of.

"I have been learning estate management from your father," he confided. "Things I should have learned in my youth from my own father. But, alas, I'd thought there would always be more time, another day with him present to learn all I needed."

"That is certainly something I understand."

They fell silent as their slow progress through the grove brought them to the edge of the trees. If they traversed a few more paces, they'd be visible from the back terrace of his townhouse.

Easily, he turned them about to face back toward the alley and their waiting carriage.

Daniel wasn't ready to share Lettie just yet—nor return to his carriage.

Could he stall a few more minutes?

"My how the trees have grown!" She halted before a particularly thick, tall tree and looked up, shielding her eyes from the sun overhead. "I truly cannot believe we once climbed these things—without a broken bone or scratch resulting."

Daniel took in the sheer size of the trees, as well. They'd grown, their fruit falling from their limbs, and new saplings taking root. As some trees aged and decayed, others grew tall and strong to take their place.

Had he and Lettie aged—decaying as the years passed?

He'd like to think that neither of them were worse for wear due to the years passing, but wiser and stronger than they'd once been.

"Have you thought of what life holds for you next, Lettie?" Again, he thought he'd never tire of saying her name aloud.

"I have only been in town a week," she said, resuming their slow walk. Dried leaves crackled and crumbled with each of their footfalls. "But I will confess the thought of returning to society is as daunting as it was when I first arrived home."

"There are some things time cannot heal, that it is not meant to heal." Daniel had no idea what made him speak those exact words, but when Lettie moved closer, burrowing into his side, Daniel suspected he'd said what she needed to hear. "We can only live one day at a time and hope the things that can never heal at least diminish in size."

Lettie sighed, and Daniel felt the tension drain from her as they made their way back through the gate and to the carriage.

"Thank you for bringing me here," she said, as he assisted her into the open-air conveyance.

"You are welcome to return whenever the need arises." Daniel took his seat and called to the coachman to continue on to Bond Street, though every inch of him screamed to remain in their small, secluded grove, where the harsh realities of life could not reach them.

Chapter Eleven

They arrived at the modiste with only moments to spare as she and Daniel bustled through the door. She was certain Daniel hadn't realized the impact his words had had on her—not all things are meant to heal. Maybe the wounds of her past would never heal. If they didn't, then it was up to her to patch and bandage them well enough that the pain and visible wounds were not obvious to those surrounding her.

For not the first time, she experienced the security of having Daniel close. The feeling that as long as he was near, nothing bad could happen to her.

It had been a long week since her arrival in London, and she hadn't seen Daniel after that first day. He was giving her ample time, and while she appreciated that greatly, her sense of loneliness was all-consuming as the nightmares no longer waited for nightfall to attack.

Curse her, but she'd missed Daniel since she'd wed Gregory.

She had no right to long for him, no right to claim his time, and certainly no right to ask anything of a man she'd betrayed. Though she'd done it in the name of love, mattered naught.

"Hold still, my lady," the modiste said. "Only a few more pins, and I shall be done."

She shook her head to clear her wayward thoughts and stood perfectly still as the modiste slipped another pin into the pre-fashioned gown she was fitting to her exact size. The three-part mirror caught Lettie from several angles, and her skin appeared pale next to the ebony muslin. She'd selected this pattern as opposed to the calico material for the soft way it hugged her and draped gracefully to the floor where one of the modiste's helpers pinned the hem.

The extravagant bolt of fabric could be traded for enough materials to outfit an entire foot battalion. Lettie pushed down her contrition, knowing if she did not select at least a half-dozen gowns, her mother would likely purchase dresses for her made from far more lavish silks and satins.

"I will return in a moment," the modiste called, clucking for her helper to follow as she departed the back fitting room, exiting through the curtain that separated this room from the front of the shop.

Lettie glanced back at her reflection—her skin had lost its sun-kissed coloring, her hair was growing back but at odd angles, and her face was far thinner, almost gaunt, from many hours of labor and not enough rest and sustenance. She was a mere shell of the woman she'd been during her debut Season. A chuckle from the front room drew Lettie's attention.

When the modiste had departed the room, she'd pushed the curtain aside, affording Lettie a glimpse of the front of the store. Daniel sat where she'd left him almost two hours prior. His continued presence wasn't necessary, and Lettie had begged him to depart and return for her later; however, he'd insisted on remaining in case she needed anything.

He'd done far more than was necessary. It was as if he were determined to continue their association and pick up where they'd left off. Well, not exactly where they'd left off since that would mean her breaking off their betrothal, and him so deep in his cups he hadn't a care he still had another woman's perfume clinging to him.

No, this was a different man than the one she'd left six years before.

This Daniel hadn't so much as accepted a goblet of dinner wine on her first night back. This Daniel listened to her when she spoke. This Daniel thought of what would put her at ease. This Daniel was charming, sympathetic, and attentive.

All things he hadn't been six years ago.

Another change, possibly the most apparent, was his hooded demeanor. He'd suspected she suffered from harrowing nightmares, but how could a gentleman of his caliber know of such things? He'd never been a soldier, never favored manual labor or dock work, and certainly, the hardships of the lower class were unknown to him; yet, still, they'd found a kinship and understanding Lettie had thought disappeared long ago, never to be rediscovered.

She struggled to process his kindness. She'd deserted him shortly before they were to wed. She'd brought shame and disgrace on both his family and hers, and then she'd fled England, leaving him to deal with the mess she'd created.

Even after all that, he sat patiently in the modiste's store front and waited for her to finish. He'd offered to escort her to keep the duchess from selecting patterns and fabrics not to Lettie's tastes.

Daniel owed her nothing.

Lettie owed *him* everything.

He glanced up from the newspaper he was reading and met her stare. He gave her a warm grin, making him all the more handsome as he pushed a lock of black hair from his eyes. For a moment, he appeared the young lord she remembered, unburdened by life and circumstances…and her heart fluttered. Once upon a time, Lettie had looked forward to wedding Daniel, starting a family, and spending their lives together.

She averted her eyes, conflicted by her colliding emotions.

For the past several months, she'd been in deep mourning for Gregory. Though it had taken only a day back in London for her emotions to betray her, and for thoughts of Daniel and their past to take over.

Certainly, Daniel was a handsome lord, but she had no right to notice. Her heart should not flutter at the sight of him. Her pulse should never quicken at the mere thought of his embrace. It was the ultimate disloyalty to Gregory and the love they'd shared.

The modiste, with her helper fast behind her, reentered the room, pulling the curtain shut and blessedly blocking Daniel from view. Lettie's cheeks reddened with shame at her lapse.

"Lady Colette," the modiste said, rushing forward with a bolt of fine velvet draped over her arm, proudly displaying it to her. "This just arrived yesterday. While it is not black or dark grey, I think it would suit in case you have occasion to wear it."

Lettie reached out her hand, tentatively caressing the soft velvet. The material was so dark it almost appeared black, yet is was midnight blue. How the color was achieved was beyond Lettie's comprehension.

"It is beautiful," she sighed. "But, truly, I have no use for a gown made of such a fine velvet."

"Your mother sent word that I must prepare at least one gown in a hue besides black and grey. If I displease the duchess, she will refuse my tab." She pushed the material closer for Lettie to inspect. "It is of the highest quality, my lady."

Lettie glanced from the velvet to the modiste and back again. How to explain the quality wasn't what caused her hesitation? It was the indulgence of purchasing a gown of such worth. Soldiers slept on the ground with nothing but their worn coat for warmth. Women who devoted their lives to their husbands and military service suffered a lack of food, heat, and shelter. She'd even assisted with the birth of a babe in camp before journeying to Waterloo. All those people suffered while Lettie was making trivial decisions about accepting a gown of crushed velvet or insisting on dresses made from less fashionable fabrics such as jacquard.

She glanced at the small pile of muslin she'd already selected for several gowns, and then down at the fine black frock she wore before turning back to the modiste.

The older woman's eyes pleaded with Lettie to accept the velvet.

With a groan, Lettie nodded.

"Wonderful, my lady," the modiste said, handing the velvet to her assistant and mumbling a few quick orders. "I think that will be sufficient. Patterns and materials have been designated. I will have this gown altered and delivered by this evening with the rest to follow within the week."

"Do take your time," Lettie argued. "I am in no need of the gowns for some time still."

"It is no trouble." With a reassuring smile, she continued. "It only needs to be taken in at the waist and the hem raised. It should take no more than an hour to accomplish."

"You are too kind." Lettie glanced back at the mirror. This was the first new gown she'd had in over four years. "You do fine work."

"Thank you, my lady." The woman's cheeks reddened at the compliment. "If there is nothing more you need, I will assist you out of this dress and help you back into your own gown."

The modiste's nimble fingers quickly unbuttoned the back of her new gown, careful not to disturb the pins placed for taking in the waist.

Within moments, Lettie was again wearing the gown she'd arrived in as she collected her bonnet and handbag.

"Is there anything else I can have made?"

"I think two bonnets to match the gowns. If it is not too much trouble." The modiste was the first person she'd encountered in London who hadn't winced at the sight of her shortened locks. "Nothing fancy, mind you, but something until my hair grows a bit. Oh, and gloves. I am in desperate need of gloves."

"There is no need to explain." The modiste gave her a pitying smile and patted her arm. "I will send the bonnets and gloves with the gowns."

"Thank you, again." Lettie securely tied the string on her bonnet under her chin and made her way to the front of the store where Daniel still waited.

When she entered, he jumped to his feet and set the newspaper he'd been reading aside. "Are you ready to depart?"

Several hours in a woman's clothing shop would likely put any man on edge.

"I am finished." Lettie retrieved her lone pair of gloves from her handbag and slipped them on. "Thank you again for escorting me. It would have been a trying afternoon with my mother."

"It is my pleasure, Lady Lettie." He held out his arm.

With a confident smile, Lettie set her hand in the crook of his arm.

The door swung open before Daniel reached for it, and a man walked in, his auburn hair catching the late-afternoon light. Lettie caught sight of Daniel's carriage waiting at the curb beyond, and suddenly, she was exhausted. She could walk for hours with a heavy pack on her back or work three days straight tending the wounded; however, a few hours being fitted for new gowns had withdrawn all the energy from her.

"Danny Boy!" the man shouted with a chuckle. Daniel's arm tensed, and he halted but made no move to turn and face the man who'd entered the shop. "I can't believe my eyes. It is you!"

"Lord Gable," Daniel said by way of greeting as he turned to face the man, releasing Lettie's arm and stepping in front of her. "I was unaware you favored women's fashion."

Lettie attempted to peek around Daniel, but he was too quick and sidestepped to block her view. Was he embarrassed to be seen with Lettie on his arm?

Maybe she was not so far off with her sense that he hid something from her—the thing that had brought about such a drastic change in him.

"No, no," Gable said. "I am only collecting a gown for my mistress…a feisty golden-haired siren, Amberlyn. You remember her from the playhouse, do you not?" Daniel didn't so much as nod to the man. "Oh, well, you have been absent for several months, but the woman is going to be the death of me—I swear the things she can do with her legs…"

Gable sighed, not bothering to finish the statement.

As if Daniel were more than capable of envisioning exactly what the man meant.

Lettie was not unaware of the pleasure shared between a man and a woman. Though speaking of such things publicly was highly indecorous. That a lady was present made Gable's statement all the more unsettling.

"Ah, well. Who do you have with you, Danny Boy?" Gable stepped around Daniel and grasped Lettie's hand, bringing it to his lips.

She could have sworn Daniel growled beside her.

"And who might you be, you tiny minx?" Gable purred as Lettie pulled her hand back from his clammy touch, the heat and moisture felt even through her gloves. "You must be the reason Danny hasn't been much for fun of late."

Lettie swallowed, glancing sideways at Daniel.

He did not smile nor join in the revelry with Gable, though neither did he step forward to make a proper introduction.

"I am Lady Lettie Hughes, my lord," Lettie said, giving a curtsy. "But I am afraid it is not I keeping Lord Linwood from any merriment."

"Oh, is that true?" Gable looked from Lettie back to Daniel. "Well, you must join me tonight. I am hosting a card game, and, well, *other* entertainments."

Daniel's eyes flashed, finally settling on Gable. "I am otherwise occupied this evening."

Gable took Lettie in from head to toe, a lecherous grin settling. "I expect you are; however, the invitation stands." Gable kept his stare trained on her. "Bring Lady Lettie Hughes with you, Danny Boy. But remember, clothing is always optional in my home."

Lettie gasped but had no opportunity to rebuff the man's insinuation.

With a tug, Daniel pulled the door wide and steered her out of the store.

"She must be quite the pleasure pot to keep you from the gaming hells, Danny Boy!"

Lord Gable's riotous laughter could be heard as Daniel's coachman assisted her into the waiting carriage.

The quick pace pushed the breath from Lettie's lungs as she all but fell on her seat, a scathing retort at the ready.

"Wait here, I will return momentarily." Daniel's eyes dared her to move an inch, their intensity kept Lettie frozen in her seat as he pivoted and made his way back into the shop.

She careened her neck to see inside, but the draperies in the front window made it impossible.

True to his word, Daniel exited the shop after only a few minutes, pushing his black hair from his face before entering the carriage.

Daniel sat across from her, his lips taut and his shoulders stiff with tension.

The words died before making it past her lips.

"I apologize for Lord Gable's inappropriate comments." He called to his driver to be off and settled in to gaze out the window as they made their way back to her family's townhouse.

The man meant to offer no other explanation for the scandalous encounter.

Lettie's temper flared red-hot. "Did that man think me to be your—" the word stuck in her throat, but she pushed it out, needing an answer, "your paramour? A kept woman?" Her voice rose with each word until her final question was little more than a shrill screech. "Your courtesan?"

Her fury only increased when he remained silent, giving her not even the satisfaction of a bogus explanation.

"Did you think because I am a widow, I would fall into your bed without benefit of any future promises? Is that why you've been so kind to me, taking me to a place I favored in the past, even after everything I did to you when I wed Gregory?"

That finally captured his attention. "I said I would never force you into any arrangement—betrothal or otherwise."

"But you were hoping I'd fall willingly into my place as your mistress, the sad, pathetic, aging widow that I am?"

His eyes flared as hot as her temper. "Of course, not. Do not be obtuse, Lettie."

She leaned forward, laying her arms across her chest. "Never in my twenty-six years have I ever been obtuse—except in this moment, not realizing the roguish ways you've taken to and how far you've truly fallen. You are not the boy I grew up with."

"You are correct, my lady, I am not a boy. I have not been for many years," he hissed, matching her pose and bringing their faces so close their noses nearly touched. "And my personal life is none of your concern. Especially the years following your flight from London and marriage to another. Do not dare cast stones at my decisions."

He was a rakehell. A rascal. His benevolence surely feigned for his own benefit. She shook her head in disbelief. "You thought me so low—penniless, homeless, and without a possession to my name—I could easily be taken to your bed? Resigned to a future of being passed between men until my beauty crumbled to nothing and I perished old and alone...a spent *whore?*"

His silence was damning.

And crushed what little Lettie had been able to piece back together from her life before the war. She'd thought seeing unknown men die on a field covered in blood and weaponry was difficult. She'd assumed tending the wounded and caring for the permanently disfigured was a fate no person should have to witness. She'd mistakenly presumed her nightmares would ultimately bring her to a level so low she could not climb out.

However, this treachery was far worse than anything she'd been subjected to thus far.

Mankind was far crueler and more uncaring than she'd ever suspected. The battlefield and what came with it was expected, but how was she to know her enemy when they wore the guise of an old, dear friend?

The carriage pulled to a stop in her drive, and the coachman leapt from his post and opened the door. He extended his hand to assist her down, but Lettie paused.

Staring directly into Daniel's midnight, cold eyes, her lifelong friend, silently imploring him to give her any answer but the one she'd concluded. She needed him to argue against her accusations. Tell her how wrong she was and offer some form of insight into what their confrontation with Gable had been about—and why he'd rushed Lettie from the shop as if the devil were on their heels.

Instead, he remained quiet, turning his penetrating glare toward the street beyond.

Just as he had all those years ago.

Lettie grabbed her handbag and took the coachman's offered hand, departing the carriage.

She nodded in thanks before lifting her chin and walking to her door. She would not run. She would not allow her sob to escape. She would not show him how deeply his silence wounded her.

Daniel had, in essence, pointed out yet again that she wasn't worth his time or effort.

Chapter Twelve

Lettie pressed her hands to her ears in an attempt to block out the barrage of banging and clanging as men worked somewhere deep in her parents' townhouse. The noise had awoken her from a fitful sleep and sent her scurrying to work the night from her eyes and get dressed.

The sounds echoed through the entire house, bouncing off the walls and rattling the windowpanes. The men appeared to be working on the second floor, for the sound increased as she made her way to her father's study, situated on the ground floor and overlooking the back gardens. The noise was directly over her head as she paused before a slightly ajar door—even over the loud workmen above, Lettie could hear her mother and father speaking…along with another familiar voice.

Daniel.

He'd called her obtuse, yet it seemed to be he who did not understand that his continued attendance in her house was unwanted. Yet, he'd still arrived almost every day since her return, though she'd avoided him over the past several days following their argument after her appointment at the modiste's shop.

Lettie leaned close, trying to discern what they spoke of over the commotion above; only a jumble of words, a raised voice, and the sound of pacing greeted her.

"You must insist, your grace," her mother demanded.

"The dowry will be yours," her father countered.

"I have promised Lady Colette I will not—" Daniel's voice was inaudible, the din of the workmen cutting off his reply.

But she'd heard enough to know they spoke of her. Her future. Her life. Everything that should be *her* decision.

They discussed it behind closed doors as if Lettie had no say in the matter.

Maybe she shouldn't have any say in her future. She could barely keep her present within her grasp as the past always threatened to take over; as it did now. A hammering sounded above stairs, pulling her out of Carrolton House and placing her back in camp. The noise of soldiers breaking down their roughly built camp as they prepared to leave the peninsular and travel to their next battle assignment rang as the hammer continued above. Lettie remembered hastily packing all her medical supplies—having to leave behind a good portion of what she'd managed to collect in their rush— and the sound of injured men being moved from cots and set upon the hard, cold ground. They would either gain their feet or be left behind.

Lettie leaned against the wall outside the study, her legs trembling beneath her as she relived that day. The sounds of cannons and musket fire were absent. Their regiment leader shouted nonstop orders. Lettie had carried both her and Gregory's belongings, allowing him to assist a wounded soldier.

The mere remembrance of that day filled Lettie with exhaustion—bone deep, soul-crushing exhaustion. At her back, the wall vibrated from the continued work, and she pressed her hands to her ears once more to drown out the noise as she squeezed her eyes shut, begging herself to return to the present.

"Lady Lettie?" Daniel's hand settled on her shoulder, and she pulled away. "Are you all right?"

"I am fine. Could not be better, in fact." Lettie shuffled on wavering legs away from Daniel. She hadn't come face-to-face with him since their tiff, and at the moment, her head pounded and swirled far too much to string together a proper retort. "I am here to speak with my parents, but I can return to my room until your meeting is complete."

He slipped an envelope into his jacket pocket before continuing; and Lettie longed to ask what business they'd been attending to—besides usurping her future. However, she was hesitant to admit that she'd been eavesdropping on their conversation.

"May I call on you later for a turn in Hyde Park?" His expression remained blank, but Lettie noted the spark in his eyes and his tense shoulders. "Or possibly on the morrow, if that suits better?"

She'd seen this before. Daniel had hope she would accept his offer and put behind them what had happened; but that could not be. There was more she longed to know, and much she didn't understand.

"I must decline, your grace," Lettie mumbled, glancing to the now open door of her father's study. "My gowns have yet to be delivered, and my mother would likely perish if I left the house in a state of disarray."

It was a lie. The modiste had been sending her commissioned wardrobe to Carrolton House as the pieces where completed. She was simply not prepared for another afternoon in Daniel's company—one moment it was as if no time had passed, as if she'd never wed another, and as if Daniel hadn't been hurt by her actions. While the next, he was clearly hiding something from her. Lettie could not organize her thinking enough to grasp what it was.

"However, thank you for your kind offer." Lettie lowered her eyes to the floor at his feet and sank into a curtsey. "I will meet with my parents now."

He'd been dismissed, and he knew it. "Do have a pleasant afternoon, my lady. Please send word if you are in need of anything."

"Of course."

With a curt bow, he pivoted and stalked down the hall toward the foyer. The banging and pounding above drowned out his footfalls before he was out of sight.

Lettie turned to her father's study and stepped into the room. "Good day, Mother, Father," she said a bit too boisterously as she threw her shoulders back in feigned confidence. "What in heavens is all the commotion?"

"Aw, good day, my dear," her father said in greeting, but did not stand from behind his desk. "You are looking well rested." It was a lie, but Lettie allowed the comment to pass unaddressed. "As far as what is happening above, your mother has decided my library does not need so many—ah, books or bookshelves."

A library with too many books? She'd never heard of such a ridiculous thing.

Lettie took a seat across from her mother on a low lounge.

"Yes, the room has become dark and crowded—besides, your father doesn't look at any of those old things anyways. It is only another room overrun by dust." The duchess shook her head—as if she'd ever in her life tidied a room or knew the labor necessary to keep a pristine house. "Tea, Colette?"

That name again. Her mother must see her cringe each time she addressed Lettie by her given name. "Thank you, Mother."

"Now, it has come to my attention that you have not left the house since your modiste appointment," her mother mused, handing Lettie a teacup.

"That is correct." She'd been able to blame her unfit wardrobe until now, but dresses had arrived, and even women in mourning did not stay secluded for the entire year. "I fear I am not ready to go out in public as yet."

"Poppycock, my daughter." The earl's head popped up from the pages he'd been inspecting behind his desk. And to think, Lettie hadn't thought he paid attention to the conversation around him. "Fresh air will do you good."

Lettie had had fresh air, in fact, she'd had enough fresh air to last her a lifetime as she'd traveled home from Waterloo—it hadn't helped to clear her mind nor ease the pain that continued to burrow deep within her.

Still, before she'd wed Gregory, she'd been her father's cherished daughter. Maybe, one day, she would make him proud once more. "I will take a turn in the gardens today. I promise." She took a sip of tea. Her delicate cup clanked against the saucer when her hands trembled.

Settling the hand-painted cup on the table beside her, Lettie threaded her fingers together to halt their shiver.

The duchess's brow rose, obviously noting Lettie's unease. "I think she needs more than fresh air, husband." Her mother took a sip from her own teacup, her hands never wavering. "I think it is past time she put all this war nonsense behind her—forget about it all—and look to the future."

"Mother, I do not think—"

"That's just it, girl, which is the problem." The duchess shook her head with regret. "But you think *too* much. Dwell, fret, and fear…not good for the soul, I tell you."

"What is not good for my soul is being made to forget the past, act as if it didn't happen." Lettie's brow pulled together. She'd rarely confronted her mother, except for the day she and Lord Linwood had broken their betrothal. "I was married…for six years. I saw many gruesome things during wartime, and I held soldiers as they died. That stain, that burden, never releases a person. It never diminished. It haunts me, day and night."

She looked to her father, seeing a spark of understand fill him only to be distinguished when her mother sighed.

This was all her mother's doing.

"I can see the change in you, my daughter, but we—your mother and I...and Lord Linwood—are at a loss for how to help you. We are doing our best, though we may miss the mark often." He stood and came to sit next to her, setting his arm around her shoulders. Immediately, Lettie was a child again, wrapped in her father's protective embrace.

He would help her. He would understand. He had to.

"Now, hurry to your room and change into a new, pretty gown...you will feel much better in a fancy dress. We will dine shortly." He pulled away from her and patted her hand, at the same time a pit grew in her stomach.

Her father didn't understand at all. He was pacifying her, telling her what she longed to hear, and all the while hoping she fell back into her old, youthful ways.

Lettie stood. "You are correct; I think it best I retire before our meal."

"Yes, and do don one of the gowns that arrived today." Her mother took hold of her needlework that had lain unnoticed at her side. "I grow tired of seeing you garbed in rags."

"Of course, Mother." Lettie nodded and quickly fled the room. At some point, the men had stopped working above, but Lettie's head still ached.

"Barclay, I think our decision to bring the *ton* to her was very wise." Her mother's final words chased her down the hall.

Chapter Thirteen

Daniel regained his seat behind his massive mahogany desk as his solicitor closed the door after his departure. He threw a quick glance at the sideboard littered with bottles, and then back to the tumbler of port sitting on the far edge of his desk—untouched by his man of business. Maybe just a sip. To take the edge off.

His body had been tight with apprehension since he'd gone back into the modiste's shop to confront Gable.

Daniel had demanded Phineas draft a note grand enough to settle on Charlie's family so that the boy's mother and sisters would never go hungry again. To his surprise, the funds with a letter attached, had arrived at Daniel's solicitor's office that very morning.

It was something Daniel should have taken care of immediately, instead of acting as if it had never happened.

But now that business had been handled, he was again without something to occupy his mind.

It had been two days since he'd stumbled upon Lettie outside her father's study door after her parents had made it clear he was to pursue their daughter with renewed vigor. Blast it all, he damn well wanted to pursue her, though not at Lord and Lady Percival's insistence.

If—when—he decided to make his intentions known to Lettie, it would be because it was his decision, not due to pressure from others.

From the dire expression she'd held the other day, he knew for certain she was not ready. Was not ready to forget the past, was not ready to mingle in society, and was not ready to believe there was hope for her future.

Daniel was determined to give her exactly that…hope.

He pulled the invitation from the drawer at his left. He didn't need to open it to know what it said. The time he'd spent studying the note, reading Lady Percival's neat, controlled writing, told Daniel all he needed to know: if Lettie were determined to deny her parents what they sought, they would invite whom they desired to Carrolton House to drag her out into society, no matter the fuss she gave.

You are cordially invited to attend a dinner party at
Carrolton House to welcome Lady Colette home.

Shoving the letter back in the drawer, Daniel scrubbed his hands down his face as he leaned back in his chair.

Who else had been invited?

In all likelihood, they'd invited other eligible lords, others to contend for her hand, if Daniel did not fall in line and capture Lettie's notice before long. The simple fact was, Lettie deserved a man far more noble than he, and Daniel understood why she pushed him away. He'd let her go all those years ago for that exact reason: she deserved a man who loved her above all else.

At the time, Daniel had only cared about himself and what pleased him. What had lifted him from the black haze of despair he'd fallen into after his father's passing. Lettie and their courtship hadn't been enough to pull him from the murky depths of sorrow—or maybe she had, and it was he who hadn't given her ample opportunity to try. Regardless, she'd deserved a devoted man—a gentleman who woke every morning to please her, to cherish her, and to protect her.

Damn it all, but he was that man.

Had they forewarned Lettie? Daniel highly doubted it, or she would have put an end to the farce long before the invitations had been sent.

If he couldn't convince Lord and Lady Percival to stop the meal, then he'd be there to protect Lettie. No matter what she said or how angry she was with him, he owed her that much. She needed him, and Daniel would not disappoint her again.

So, she may be avoiding him, telling him he wasn't wanted, but he knew differently.

One day, she would realize this—and he would be there at her side, proving that he had changed. He was not the man she accused him of being. He would never deny his flaws and faults, but that was not the man he was now.

It had taken years of bitterness and hurt to realize that while it had pained him to let her go, it was only in doing so that she'd become the woman she was today. Hell, he was proud of her, and of himself for sacrificing his happiness for her.

While Lettie had changed, so had Daniel. He was wiser, and now knew what would truly make him happy, though not in his many vivid dreams had he imagined Lettie would come back to England—and him.

He pushed back his chair and stood.

The time had come to prepare, and if he'd learned anything about Lettie, she was not one to be kept waiting.

# # #

Daniel paused outside the parlor as another moment of doubt overtook him. He shouldn't have come. It would have been wise for him to send his regrets to Lord and Lady Percival; however, Daniel was unwilling to let Lettie face a parlor full of people without an ally by her side.

Damn it. He should have been honest with her days ago. It was because of him they'd fought. Honestly, he could not rightfully, and in good conscience, blame everything that had transpired on Lord Gable.

Daniel was who he was. That he'd worked hard to do away with his roguish ways, banish his rakehell tendencies that had become almost second nature over the long years alone, should win him some reward. A prize of leniency at the very least.

Lettie hadn't any notion how far he'd fallen into debauchery. Although, at present, he suspected she was learning.

And he couldn't be frightened to face her head-on and explain his past with no excuses or rationalizations. She deserved honesty while Daniel deserved her scorn. Their brief time walking among the grove of plum trees only reinforced her innocence in everything and his culpability.

A bubble of female laughter floated from the room beyond the closed door, though Lettie's light laugh was noticeably missing from the choir.

He took a deep breath, straightened his neckcloth, and patted his hair into place. "I'm ready."

"Very good, your grace," the butler pushed the door wide with a flourish, revealing a room cluttered with women he adamantly avoided, and men who'd aged out of their wild ways years before. "Ladies and gentlemen, may I present the Duke of Linwood."

Daniel instantly spotted Lettie, gowned in a dress of pure black, the only adornment the velvet trim along the hem and neckline, which reached to her chin. She appeared every inch the widow she was. By the way the females gathered around her squawked and giggled, he was the only one to notice.

She was stunning, captivating, and enthralling all at the same time. Her mourning shroud hid more than the pain of her past, but lent an air of mystery to her person.

The duchess had settled on the grand idea to host this party in hopes that Lettie would embrace her old life in town, reconnect with her dear friends, and eventually, do away with her mourning garb before the Season ended. It was a risky tactic on their part, and no doubt, Lettie would see clear through their scam. If not, Daniel was more than willing to play her companion for the evening and steer the conversation in a direction that would not cause her any pain.

Lettie may not want him there, but she damn well *needed* him there. Or maybe he only deluded himself and it was he who needed her.

"Good evening," Daniel said, nodding to several men he'd met on occasion before moving to Lettie's side. Her guests were occupied, completely missing she did not offer him any greeting. He'd count his blessings that she didn't outright throw him from the room. "Lady Lettie. Thank you for inviting me this evening."

She did not refute his insinuation that it had been her idea to invite him, but instead, set her sights on being an acceptable hostess. "May I introduce Lady Buttomcoup, Lady Alsoup, and Lady Haunton. We all attended our first Season together."

"No gentleman with any sense could forget the year London was presented with the finest crop of debutantes ever to grace a ballroom." Daniel bowed low as the women tittered behind their fans at his outlandish greeting.

"Hear, hear, Linwood!" the men, clustered by the sideboard, called in agreement as they raised their glasses in salute to their wives.

"What will you have, your grace?" Lord Alsoup motioned to the grand display of decanters on the sideboard and waggled his brows as if they were nothing more than a group of University gents nipping a few pulls from one of their father's treasured liquor cabinet.

Daniel waved him off with a shake of his head. He needed to keep his wits about him if he were going to assist Lettie in making it through the evening. "It is a pleasure to see you all again," he said to the gathering at large.

The women giggled once more, and Lettie winced as they returned to their conversation. Namely, painted cotton gowns imported from India—Lady Buttomcoup insisted they'd fallen out of fashion twenty years before, while Lady Haunton adamantly disagreed. Lettie was called on to make her worldly edict on the matter.

She rubbed her brow. The women thought she pondered the subject, while Daniel suspected Lettie had developed a headache and was certainly in need of a drink—far more than he.

Leaning close, he whispered, "May I offer you refreshments, my lady?"

Her back stiffened but she nodded in agreement, still avoiding eye contact with him.

She had yet to forgive him.

A bottle of sherry sat on the sideboard, and Daniel quickly poured her a healthy portion. If it didn't help relieve her headache, at least it would drown out the incessant chatter.

"What have you been up to, Linwood?" the Earl of Haunton inquired. "We haven't seen you much at White's or Tattersall's. Thought you'd retired to the country or some other outrageous thing."

Daniel only knew the trio of men in passing, but they normally stayed close, presumably because their wives were friends. "No, no," Daniel said with a pretentious chuckle. "I would not think of leaving the delights of London, especially during the Season."

The men shared a knowing look. What they thought they knew wasn't apparent to Daniel.

"Now that Lady Lettie is back in London, we hope to see you more frequency." It was Buttomcoup who spoke, petting his rounded paunch as he did. He appeared a caricature from that tawdry gossip rag the Duchess of Essex always kept lying around.

Exactly how frequently they expected to see him was uncertain; however, since he'd only spoken with the man on two occasions—that he could recall—he wasn't worried about them demanding much of his time.

"Certainly." He tilted his head in Lettie's direction. "If you will excuse me, I must bring my lady her sherry."

"Of course, of course." Alsoup waved him off.

"We all know how women get if their drink is not brought with all due haste," Haunton chimed in.

"Would be awful to irk Lady Lettie so soon," Buttomcoup jested.

The three men found their comments highly amusing as they all chortled in unison.

It seemed a gaggle of men was just as daunting and annoying as a flock of women.

He wondered if they'd be surprised or impressed to know he'd already angered her.

With a conspiratorial grin for the men, he moved back toward Lettie. Her hands were clutched in her lap, knuckles white from wringing her kerchief. It seemed the other women were oblivious to her discomfort, none of the three noticing her unease.

"Lettie," Lady Buttomcoup gushed. "You certainly must speak with your parents and request to journey with us to Bath. We make the trip every year. The children love the hot baths. And, of course, we enjoy several weeks together."

The trio nodded in unison, as their husbands had, appearing much like a group of bobbing pigeons walking through Hyde Park looking for food scraps.

Lettie blanched at the mention of children.

"Not that you don't already know the excitement of traveling," Lady Haunton exclaimed, reaching out to touch Lettie's clenched hands. "Your mother tells us you and your late husband journeyed extensively during your marriage."

"Ummm…" Lettie allowed a hint of a smile at the mention of Gregory. "Yes, though I would not say it was exciting in any way. We traveled with a large group of soldiers."

"And France?" Lady Alsoup gushed loudly enough for her husband to hear. "I have wanted to visit Paris for some time."

"Devine," Lord Alsoup called from the sideboard. "As soon as the children are old enough for that kind of journey, we will go."

"You truly must instruct me on all the finest places to visit when there," the lady pouted. "Though it may be years before Lord Alsoup will take me."

"I fear I will be of little assistance, Devine," Lettie sighed. "My travels were not for pleasure. It was my duty to cook, mend clothing, and tend to the wounded. Now, if one of the children falls and injures their arm, I can set and bind a broken limb as well as any doctor."

It was Lettie's attempt at setting the women straight, but also joking so no one took offense.

All three women paused long enough to gauge if Lettie jested or not.

When a hesitant laugh broke the silence, Daniel supposed they truly believed her journey with the British soldiers to fight off Napoleon's troops was nothing more than a jaunt to the wilds of Northumberland.

Lettie's shoulders tensed as the women continued to cackle.

Daniel watched as she glanced at the door—her only escape. She was close to fleeing. He could see it in the way her shoulders had gone from tense to caving in on her.

"Just wait until word spreads that you are back in London—and ready to make a perfect match!" Lady Alsoup clapped with eagerness. "It will be as grand as our first Season."

Grand as their first Season? Daniel had barely made it through Lettie's debut Season. She'd been chased by every available lord, and many who weren't. He'd been made to stay in the shadows as she took her place in the spotlight, but at the end of each night, she'd left on his arm.

Would things be different if she re-entered society?

Thankfully, the butler stepped back into the room at that moment. "Dinner will be served now. Lord and Lady Percival will meet you all in the dining hall. This way, please."

Buttomcoup, Alsoup, and Haunton each moved to assist their wives with standing and offered their arms, following the butler from the room, leaving Daniel and Lettie alone.

He offered his arm, and she stood, resting her hand at his elbow.

"I am sorry about what happened at the modiste's." It was no more than a sigh. He'd never been adept at apologizing for his actions, though, admittedly, he owed her further explanation. Acknowledging his shortcomings after all these years and losing her a second time would be more damaging than the first time.

Her chin notched upward. "Did you know about this?"

If he admitted that he did, she'd be livid, but lying wasn't an option either. Their time together had been rocky enough without him further angering her with deception. "I received an invitation the day I saw you outside your father's study. With a note from the duchess. I know you are cross with me—"

"Then why did you come?" She turned accusing eyes on him. "This entire gathering is a farce. I am not the woman I was six years ago. I will never be that woman again. I have seen too much, experienced more than any woman should. Inviting my past to confront me, their happiness and joy on display, will do nothing but push me further away from them—and my parents."

Lady Haunton poked her head back into the room. "Are you coming, Lettie?"

"Yes. I will be there momentarily. I need to freshen up a bit." She turned to Daniel after Lady Haunton had disappeared. "Go and join the others. I need a moment alone if you don't mind."

He started to argue, to tell her he'd wait with her until she was ready to join everyone, but she held up a finger, silencing any protest. "Please." Her voice cracked and tears glistened in her eyes.

She didn't want him to see her cry. That was something Daniel understood well.

"Very well, but if you do not arrive presently, I will come looking for you," he warned.

Chapter Fourteen

Lettie only exhaled when she closed the door to her bedchambers, blocking out the laughter and conversation drifting up from below. Everyone was having a marvelous time and entirely unaware of her heart thumping wildly in her chest. Something was wrong with her—something that had come about since witnessing all she had on the battlefield. She'd never be as she was before. It was no longer within her capacity to enjoy a gathering or sit down to a meal with others.

Every mention of family, children, home—normalcy—triggered a deep-seated response within her she was unable to control. Her lungs froze, her heart pulsed erratically, and words failed her. After years of flintlocks, muskets, cannons sounding at close distances, men shouting orders outside her medical tent, and the cries of agony as soldiers littered every available spot, the nonsense and coquettish chatter of the women certainly shouldn't have sent her into a panic. But it had. And Lettie feared it was her newfound reality.

And with each day that passed, her mind became more and more jumbled—the pieces of a complex puzzled which were fated never to fit together.

Polite society was no place for her. Her disposition and state of mind were far too unpredictable. She was doomed to embarrass her family—and disgrace herself.

A single candle stood lit on her washstand, her bed turned down for the night, and a pristine white nightshift laid across her rose-colored eyelet bedspread.

She'd spent years surrounded by activity: soldiers, cannon fire, musket rounds, and wagon wheels.

Years had passed without a single moment of silence.

Now, it seemed the only place that could bring her calm was somewhere free of others.

Deafening silence.

She didn't think she'd be able to enjoy a still, quiet room again; however, neither did she delight in a salon full of inane idle chatter—fashion, travel, and then talk of family and children. All the things she'd never be capable of.

But quiet and isolation did not stop the churning of her mind. The endless nights reliving Gregory's final moments. Even her trip through the plum trees with Daniel several days ago had only given her a momentary reprieve, a glimpse at peace.

It was too much. She'd rather spend unending days tending to brave, injured soldiers than an hour surrounded by the *ton*. There had been nothing but heartache, loss, and carnage during her time away from London. Though at least with her hands occupied, her mind did not wander to things she could not speak of to anyone who hadn't witnessed the horrors firsthand. They would not understand.

Her time in the salon with the women had proven this.

She'd once counted the ladies as her closest friends, but the years and her circumstances had driven a solid wedge between them.

Her only saving grace was Daniel, which galled her.

One moment, he was the man she'd longed for him to be during their betrothal; and the next, he retreated behind a wall she could not climb over.

Days had passed, but she continued to be irate with him. Annoyed he so obviously kept something from her. But he had witnessed her shortcomings firsthand, heard all of her tawdry tales of war, and had woken her from one of her worst nightmares. Even with all that, he hadn't abandoned her to deal with the women alone. He'd even made certain she knew he still came by Carrolton House, though she'd demanded he stay away.

She'd opened up to him, yet he didn't value her enough to do the same.

Everything about him was in conflict. She knew him well, but at the same time suspected she knew nothing of him.

She'd been tempted to confess the damage and irreparable harm caused by war to the entire gathering. The immense isolation she'd felt during the last six years, though Gregory had only left her side during battle. They'd slept next to one another every night unless she had injured men to see to, and even those times, Gregory had forgone sleep to help her, gathering supplies and medicine as she needed them.

But Daniel's presence stopped her.

The women, even now enjoying a meal of delicate dishes and sweet desserts, hadn't experienced the last breath of a soldier lying prone on a gurney as they worked diligently to staunch the flow of his life blood. Or the way it felt to be greeted with the rattle of death as a man exhaled for the final time. She could not think past the differences between her and the other women. It shouldn't matter, yet it did.

Could Daniel understand the damage left behind after witnessing everything she did while at war?

Lettie's legs quaked, and she searched her room for a place to sit. The girlish white dressing table was not fit for a woman who'd seen as much crimson as Lettie had. Despite the chill of Waterloo and the unrelenting rain, her hands had been coated in warm, red blood for most of her waking hours. No amount of lye soap had removed the flakes left under her trimmed nails.

The bed was no better an option. If she took to its softness, she'd likely never gain the willpower to leave it. After years of sleeping on the hard, muddy ground, the delicate, plush, four-poster bed with its sheer drapes was more than she'd ever expected to enjoy again. Even the night before had been a restless, fitful sleep. No amount of indulgent pillows or well-sprung, straw-stuffed bedding could dispel the dreams that plagued her nights.

Her cavernous bedchambers were too tranquil— and still foreign to her even after nearly two weeks home.

It made her erratic heart rate spike once more, the sound of her thrumming blood deafening in her head.

She was uncomfortable in a boisterous group and panicky in a quiet room.

Could it be she would never again feel any sense of rightness?

Lettie needed to go to her parents—and speak with Daniel. Needed to tell them of her brokenness, beg them to take mercy on her even if they couldn't understand her turmoil. Something within her mind wasn't right. It was as if whatever connected everything in her brain had been destroyed. They needed to allow her to journey to the country, away from any prying eyes, and give her permission to implode on her own. At least then, she could shield them from her disgrace.

Grasping the lone source of light in the room, Lettie shook her head before slipping through the open door of her dressing closet. Freshly laundered and pressed gowns hung neatly and orderly, blacks fading to greys, and finally her deep midnight-blue velvet gown. Her only turn of frivolousness. She reached out and allowed her fingers to caress the fine material—the stitching perfect without a visible flaw. The dexterity of the garment certainly must have taken hours to achieve. Then again, she'd stitched wounds so tightly and precisely nary a scar was seen once the soldier healed.

Lettie placed the candle on the floor, safely away from her line of brocade slippers and hanging fabrics. Her fingers shook as she undid the row of buttons holding the front of her gown closed. Pulling her arms from the black gown she'd selected for the evening, she pushed the material down and over her waistline. The muslin pooled at her feet, leaving her clothed in only her shift and underpinnings.

A shiver coursed down her spine, and she removed the new lovely gown from its hanger. The velvet was pleasing to her touch, at odds with the sturdy, thick, coarse garb she was used to wearing.

The dress was perfect.

It would be beautiful evening attire to any other woman, but for Lettie, it was a *costume*, a mask to hide from others what lay beneath—and within her. She'd thought her rash decision to have this particular gown commissioned was a piece of her youth coming back, her flight of fancy tendencies reawakening. But, no, it was her true self, the one who had been created while witnessing the travesties of life. That was the Lettie who had had to have the gown, regardless of the cost.

Slipping the dress over her head, she let it float down her body, hugging every curve. What little curves she still possessed anyway. The only flaw she found was that it did not extend far enough to cover her shortened hair. Her costume would be complete with a matching hood.

The hem appropriately swept the floor at her feet.

Lettie reached behind her to fasten the buttons at her back. After three, she reached just above her waist and stretched but was unable to secure another. It didn't matter, she wasn't leaving her dressing closet. No one would see her with her back exposed, the front gaping loosely.

It was only rightly so.

The gown was perfection.

Lettie was the epitome of imperfection.

The finest dress, gloves, hat, and slippers would never be able to mask Lettie's flaws. It may be enough to mislead some, much as it had with her friends below; however, with time, the person she'd become would be apparent to all.

Shattered.

Fragmented.

Defective.

Unequivocally broken.

And with additional time, fractured or splintered so entirely a gust of wind would blow the remaining parts far and wide. Would her damage then affect others? Burrow deep inside those who inhaled her splintered being.

Lettie could not allow that to happen. If wearing a binding gown of rich fabric was all it took to keep the pieces together, maybe that was worth her dying inside so others didn't have to.

It was likely a blessing she was at least conscious of her defects.

She pulled the door to her dressing closet toward her, cutting off the sight of her massive bedchamber and bringing herself to face the mirror that hung on the inside of the door. The small amount of light given off from the single candle was magnified with the mirror's help, illuminating Lettie.

She gazed upon herself for the first time in many years—without her youthful trappings disguising her, without the mask of war garb hiding her weak shoulders, without the filth of the battlefield and blood of the surgical tent holding at bay her trembling, thin body.

Here, in the home of her past, she could not run from the woman she'd become.

Even if Gregory hadn't perished and they'd returned to London as a wedded couple, she still would feel out of place. The nightmares would have still come. She had no doubt.

Lettie turned to the side, noting her trim waist and high cheekbones with hollowed face below. No veil would hide the empty vastness of her eyes.

Astoundingly, she didn't want to keep hidden her deepest musings, her hurt, and her despair.

She lifted her chin. How could she ever hope to overcome it if her future was a carefully crafted lie to protect those around her? She could not expect anyone to accept her at present.

"Lettie?" The hinges on her bedchamber door squeaked, and boot steps sounded in her private space. "Are you within, my lady?"

Daniel.

She'd promised to freshen up and join them for the evening meal. It was best he learn now that all Lettie's future held was disappointment after disappointment. If he chose to renew their childhood friendship or continue on her parent's foolhardy mission to see them wed, then it was something he'd need to gain comfort with.

Broken promises.

Shattered longings.

And miserable disappointment.

"I am here," Lettie sighed, reaching forward and running her finger down the glass, tracing the face she no longer recognized as her own. Loss etched every line. Sorrow hung heavy in her brow. Even her once plump lips were little more than a frown.

His steps moved toward her small sanctuary, and Lettie pushed the door open, revealing herself, candlelight at her back.

"Your mother was going to come fetch you, but I offered assistance. She does enjoy entertaining—" His words halted when she stepped from the closet; her stare focused on the floor. "My apologies. I was unaware you were changing gowns, though I must say you've selected a superb choice."

Lettie brought her eyes to his, startled to see nothing but gentleness in his soft expression. "I will not be re-joining the party."

"I expected as much, though it is a loss to everyone below not to witness your stunning beauty in that dress." She expected his eyes to travel from her face to her toes, only pausing to take in her gaping bodice; however, his eyes never left hers, making Lettie wonder if he could see past her emptiness—and more acutely, wondering *what* he saw there. "I was against this dinner. It is far too soon, and I should have worked harder to discourage them."

"It was not your place," Lettie sighed. They were barely friends—she and Daniel—their past betrothal notwithstanding, no matter how much he tried to prove otherwise. "None of this is your fault."

"Mayhap not, yet, I endeavor to show you that I value our long friendship despite the rough trials we've faced." He pulled the bench out from her dressing table and sat. When had he turned into the pure white knight, and she the black domino?

"Why are you trying so hard to prove something?" Lettie crossed her arms to cover her less than properly gowned bosom. "You owe me nothing...less than nothing, in fact. If it is not a mistress you seek, then what? My dowry?"

She'd heard her father declare Lettie's funds his when they wed. They were so certain of the fact, they'd all but given Daniel a banknote in good faith.

He chuckled as if she'd said the most hilarious thing he'd heard in ages. Sobering, his brow rose. "Certainly you remember your parents did away with your dowry when you chose to marry a man they did not approve of."

"I was aware of that fact every day of the last six years." She'd only had the clothes on her back and the items assigned to her as the wife of a soldier. Nothing more. Not that it was Lord and Lady Percival's fault. Lettie had insisted on leaving with nothing, only her damned principles intact. "The compromise was not a total hardship. I was with the man I loved." She paused, swallowing a sob. "I still love him."

"That fact is not in dispute," Daniel consented. "I assure you, you are the expert in matters of the heart."

She ignored his remark. "However, we both know if I were to tuck tail and give in to my parents' demands to reenter society and wed—namely, you—my dowry would be reinstated, and likely tripled."

"My wealth matches, if not significantly surpasses, that of the Percival and Essex titles combined." The corner of his mouth cocked in a mocking grin. "Do you have any other arguments to prove my intentions dishonorable?"

She'd barely had any argument to start with. The need to make her his mistress hadn't rung true. If Daniel had meant to compromise her, he'd had many chances before she wed Gregory and fled England, but he had never acted anything but the gentleman. Why continue a close association with her father if he meant to defile her honor? Besides, that explanation lent no credence as to why he'd volunteered to be her nursemaid during this travesty of a dinner party.

She threw her arms wide. "I give up, Daniel. I do not understand why you seek to befriend a woman who jilted you and returned to London little more than a shell of who she once was. I am in love with a man who is gone. A piece of my heart was left on that battlefield—the rest buried with Gregory. I am a penniless widow with little drive to go on…"

She pivoted and retrieved her candle from the floor in the closet before turning to face him once more. She needed to collect her thoughts—as disjointed as her mind was—and say all that must be said. This may very well be her final chance.

"If you insist on friendship, I cannot stop you, especially with my parents aligned with you, but know that I have nothing else to give you. I do not belong here. I am not the debutante and well-raised woman I once was; the female my parents are determined to make me once more. She is dead. Buried in a grassy plain far away under a sapling. Please, I beg you." She inhaled deeply. "Please, do not expect anything more from me…I am incapable of it. I have nothing left to give."

Lettie focused on him in the dim light, scared of what she would see, but needing to show him—and herself—that she was many things, including aware of her flaws.

He stood quickly, and Lettie feared he'd leave without another word.

It would be for the best. It had to be this way.

But he closed the distance between them and pulled her against him forcing her to hurriedly put the candle down. He settled his lips against hers. Shock stiffened her back, and she pushed at his chest, though with little conviction.

His kiss…their kiss…it was…

Demanding, yet soft.

Insistent, but not punishing.

His hand settled on the back of her neck, holding her to him as if he tried to pass his strength on to her.

Did he not realize it was her remaining strength that allowed her to speak her mind, no matter how much it had hurt them both?

Her traitorous body softened and melded against his, fitting perfectly to his contours.

It only increased her awareness of his attraction.

Daniel's arousal pushed against her belly as his tongue darted out and slid across her bottom lip, severing their connection.

It was unlike any kiss she'd experienced before, holding more passion than she thought possible for any one person. And it all came from *him*—she had no desire or passion left within her.

Before this moment, Lettie was resigned to never know the passionate embrace of a man again.

As her will to push him away receded, her hands slipped around his back and pressed him to her, determined to take all he had to offer…

The consequences and disappointment be damned.

In his arms, their lips joined, she was not a broken woman. She was not living in her tragic past.

She was only Lettie.

A woman worthy of a man's embrace.

This man's embrace.

Chapter Fifteen

Their kiss was everything Daniel had thought it would be, though it should not be happening now, in bedchambers, with only a small candle for propriety, and a gown already unfastened. His hands itched to pull the dress from her body. Bloody hell, he'd wanted this since seeing her standing alone in The George. Their time in the grove had almost undone him. Blast it all, he'd wanted this moment since he was old enough to understand what the stirring in his trousers meant, or that the emptiness in his chest was when Lettie was not near.

She could not deny how well they fit against one another. Even now, he could hear their hearts beating as one.

Lettie's resistance subsided quickly and her arms locked around him, pulling him closer as their mouths danced. It was not a parry and thrust. It was not two people moving toward opposite goals. It was a complete union, both physical and emotional.

He had no designs on her wealth, her lands, nor did he have any thoughts to possess her—without the proper band nestled on her hand. He wanted all of her—mind, body, and soul.

They were always meant to be in this position: their bodies locked together as tightly as their lips, her arms encircling him as she caressed his back, and his need pressed securely between them. Lettie felt her way across his corded back, his skin flaming in each place she dragged her fingers across.

Daniel allowed his hands to roam where her shift-covered back was exposed by her undone gown. He longed to move his hands down and unfasten the remaining buttons, pushing the gown from her arms to puddle at her feet. He wanted this—needed this—however, something kept his desire under control.

If he let go and she succumbed during their moment of passion, he'd prove himself to be everything he'd begged her to believe he wasn't.

As if sensing his resolve, Lettie pulled back. Her arms fell away, and she glanced down at them as if she hadn't known they were exploring his body while her thoughts were on their kiss.

"I am a married woman, your grace," she breathed heavily, her chest heaving. Her entire body quivered and her hands trembled at her sides. The shoulder of her gown slipped down her arm, revealing her demure white shift.

His eyes followed its descent, and he reached out to tug it back onto her shoulder.

When he moved, she flinched out of reach.

"Your grace, Daniel, I…" She glanced around her bedchambers as if noting for the first time how alone they were. "I cannot. Gregory. He…"

"Shhh," Daniel soothed, reaching for her once more and righting her gown. "I understand; however, you are not a married woman. You have not been for many months. Though that does not excuse my actions. I did not seek you out with this in mind."

There was so much more he needed to tell her, but it was too soon.

And she was too raw.

Every inch of her shook as she stumbled to her dressing table bench and sank onto it.

One moment she was the confident, brave woman who'd followed her heart and committed to a life of endless hardships…and with the flip of a coin, she'd turned into the scared, anxious, crumbling woman before him. He wanted to understand her, unravel her mind, and help her create a future, whether it included him or not.

If anyone deserved a future to look forward to, it was Lettie. It was long past time she stopped sacrificing her happiness for others.

She rubbed her hands against her face, a single quiet sob filling the room.

Daniel's heart broke a bit more to see her struggling with her inner turmoil, the intangible pain locked within her.

Trembling slowly overtook her entire body.

"Lettie," he said, the hoarse whisper nearly lodging in his throat. He moved to kneel before her and pulled her hands from her face where they scrubbed harshly at some invisible stain. "Look at me."

Her eyes met his, tears pooling in their depths, ready to spill down her cheeks.

Lightly, so as not to cause her any further discomfort, he brushed the moisture away when it began to fall.

"Lettie." He would never tire of saying her name. "You make those around you better. You've made *me* a better person, even with your absence."

"How can that be when I cannot so much as get my own mind in order?" she muttered. "Everything— my thoughts and emotions—is a jumbled, disorderly mess. I cannot seem to make sense of anything."

A part of Daniel knew that getting her to talk about what was going on inside her head was the first step to healing—not only for her, but also for him. He needed to talk, share everything about what had happened in those early-morning hours of Christmastide the year prior.

"Can I ask you a question?"

She nodded, unable to speak as her chin quivered.

"Do you plan to spend your life mourning Gregory?" He wasn't sure why her answer was so important; however, he needed to know.

"I...I do not know."

"Do you think he'd want that for you?" he asked. If he'd been wise enough to wed Lettie and then had the misfortune of passing on, he'd never want her to wallow in mourning.

She brought a narrowed-eye glare to him, a spark of fire returning. Her mood shifted from despondency to assurance in the blink of an eye. "Of course, not. That is a preposterous question, yet, he is not here to direct me on how to live my life, nor tell me how to deal with his loss."

"But you have me," Daniel said with quiet confidence. He set his hands on the bench on either side of her hips. "And your parents. And three close friends. None of whom may understand what you are going through—hell, I'm unsure *I* know what you're going through—but that does not mean they care any less for you or do not want to help, though we are all struggling to discern how."

"I just want to be left alone." She broke eye contact and retreated into her shell, the barrier between them raising. "That is what I want. To be alone. Time to mourn. Space to heal."

Daniel doubted there was enough time and space for Lettie to heal without the help of those who cared for her. He was at a loss for how to get her to understand that. "We are all uncertain how to proceed, this is new territory for all of us, but one thing I do know is that Gregory would never want you to shrivel in despair and give up. There is no possibility that *you* could fall in love with a man who would expect that of you." He placed his forefinger to her chin and lifted her eyes back to his. "I am not saying you will ever find a love that compares to what you and Gregory shared; however, your husband did not fall in love with a weak woman who would be afraid to go on without him. He would want you to achieve all you'd planned to have together: a family, children, and a home full to brimming with love and laughter."

Lettie pulled her chin from his hold, and her back stiffened.

"Be the woman Gregory fell in love with six years ago. If not today, mayhap tomorrow or the next day."

The same woman Daniel had fallen in love with in his youth.

A woman who saw the best in others. A crusader for the less fortunate. A lady who did not wrap her entire existence in fine garb and fancy gloves. A nurse on the battlefields. And most importantly, Daniel's only true friend.

He needed her to be that woman again.

If she were unable to heal, what chance did that leave for Daniel to overcome his own hurt and guilt?

Chapter Sixteen

Lettie steeled her nerves, silently begging her body to stop shaking and regain the tight-laced control she'd been known for on the battlefield. She eased her grip on the bench, and feeling flooded back into her fingers, banishing the numbness and returning color to her knuckles. She only wished it were that simple to bring sensation back to the rest of her. Physically letting go was far easier than mentally and emotionally.

It would be far simpler to physically throw herself off a tall cliff than release her emotional hold on everything she'd experienced over the last six years. Then it would not matter the immense baggage she carried. It would be cast to the wind when she hit the earth below. Everything, all her worries, her remorse, her regret, and her loneliness wouldn't matter, would not hold her down.

Her heart pounded as if attempting to escape the restraints of her chest.

That was the only way Lettie could see becoming the person she once was.

Through her own demise.

Ironic that she'd need to force her hellish burdens on others and cause her own death to free herself.

Maybe letting go was not an all or nothing commitment.

She'd loved Gregory with her entire being, that would never change; however, putting their time together in a box, sealing it, and seeing what else life held for her was no meager task. It would be more difficult than throwing her life away.

But Daniel was willing to help her and be there with her through it all.

As he was doing at this very moment. He remained silent as she processed everything he'd said, but stayed before her in case she needed his support.

Where had this man been when she'd so desperately needed him to understand her in their youth? If he'd given her what she'd longed for, lending even an ear to listen, she would not have been compelled toward Gregory...a man all too willing to take her as his own. Daniel had chosen gambling and drinking over her and their betrothal.

Lettie was hesitant to forget that simple fact.

"Can I tell you a story?" His hand brushed her knee when he moved to stand.

"I find I am not in the mood for happy stories." She shifted, turning her gaze to the single candle as it neared the end of its wick. The dim room would soon be cast into total darkness. "It is difficult for me to believe that life—or at least the life I've experienced—can have any happiness or even serenity."

"This is not a happy story. There is no fairy tale ending of love, contentment, or fulfillment, though you've asked several times why I haven't wed since you left, and what has occupied me these many years." He turned away from her and paced toward her unlit hearth before pivoting and retracing his steps. "My life has not been what I wished it to be. There were no pretty moments."

His steps faltered on his final words, and he stopped, staring directly at her.

Oddly, the more she focused on Daniel, the less she noticed her trembling body. Was focusing the way to repair her mind, to draw the pieces back together and move forward?

She lifted her chin. "I have seen much worse than any story you could possibly share, Daniel." Her voice didn't waver, betraying the deep truth of the statement.

"Of that I am certain; however, it may explain how I've changed from the man I was when you called off our betrothal to who I am today." He turned away from her again.

She was unsure if he was giving her privacy while he told the story, or if the separation was for him. It didn't matter, Lettie wanted to know more no matter if it were happy or not, if only to keep her mind focused on problems that were not her own. The way her mind had easily swirled around ending her own life terrified her. Casting herself from a tall cliff—allowing body and mind to shatter completely when it hit rock bottom.

It was almost easy to feel the wind hit her face as she flung herself over the ledge.

Her heartbeat thrashed in her ears as she took a deep breath, begging her body to calm down and listen to Daniel

His story began, and his voice remained flat, detached and cold. It reminded her of the many years ago when she'd started to notice him pulling away from her and their friendship.

"It was Christmastide last year. I'd been invited to a party at Lord Gable's townhouse. It was a night of uninhibited debauchery the likes of which even I hadn't witnessed before. There was no end to the supplies of liquor, willing women, and high-stakes card games." As the story progressed, his tone turned angry and clipped. He spoke of the extreme amount of illicit activities he'd helped himself to; the way he'd stumbled to the door shortly before the sun crested on the day of celebration. With a new reserved voice, he turned back to her. "When I departed Lord Gable's home, a street urchin ran past me, one of Gable's footmen in pursuit. The boy, Charlie, had stolen from the kitchens to feed his family. This wasn't the first time; however, Gable was determined to make it the boy's last."

Lettie did not want to hear the rest of his story, but he continued anyways, his eyes locked on hers the entire time. Her stomach twisted at what could only come next, but all the same, her attention remained riveted on his words. "I tried to speak for the boy, promised Gable Charlie was sorry and that he'd never be seen on his property again, but the lord demanded I leave…without the child."

She gasped, and her inhale caught in her lungs, burning to be released but trapped all the same.

"And so, I climbed into my carriage with unsteady legs and set off for home." His head fell forward in defeat, and Lettie suspected the story did not end there. She could not have been more correct as he spoke again, his voice more hesitant than ever. "I traveled only two blocks before I called to my driver to turn around and deliver me back to Gable's. But when I pulled into the drive, Gable, his footman, and the boy were gone. Nowhere to be seen."

"Where did they go?" she breathed, her fingers clutching her crushed velvet gown.

He held up a single finger to quiet her, as though if she interrupted, he would lose the courage to continue. "As I was about to jump in my coach once more, I heard a child's weeping…and the crack of a whip. I rushed around the house as another scream disturbed the early morning. A light burned brightly in the stables. I pushed the door wide as another cry of agony and the wiz of the whip echoed off the walls of the stable."

Full body tremors overtook Lettie once more. She was stunned…speechless. She'd witnessed much at war; the death of men and many civilians, but never the unforgivable beating of a child. The men who took to the battlefields were willing and informed of the dangers they faced.

Her chest seized in pain, desperate to beg Daniel stop speaking or tell her it wasn't true.

"I called for Gable to stop, I ran to aid the boy, but I was too late." Daniel gasped, sucking down a big gulp of air and swallowing a sob. "As I entered the stable, the whip made one final arc and struck Charlie in the throat, ripping it wide. He fell back and knocked his head on a wooden post. He never regained his senses. Before the doctor could be called or the magistrate summoned, the boy perished in my arms. This is the scene that plays over and over in my nightmares." He sank to the bench next to her, and it groaned in protest at their combined weight, but he didn't leave her side as he took hold of her hand. "So, you may have witnessed much during war; however, you worked tirelessly to help those who were injured. I, on the other hand, allowed my drinking to get so far out of control I was unable to help Charlie. I fled. I froze. I didn't act in time to save him. Instead of Charlie returning home with a loaf of bread for his mother and sisters to eat on Christmas morning, I knocked on his family's door and gave them his battered and beaten body, wrapped in my evening coat. I have never told anyone this before."

He slumped beside her, leaning gently against her.

She itched to hold him, slip her arm around his shoulders and draw him ever closer to her. However, every limb of her body felt heavy, the same as she'd felt each time a soldier lay deceased when she was unable to save them.

"Daniel, Lord Gable's cruel nature was not your doing." She was at a loss for how to console him—if that was even what he needed. If his anguish were anything like hers, Daniel hadn't any idea what could help him move past Charlie's death. His words only convinced Lettie that Daniel never meant to hide his past or keep her from knowing anything, but it had been to protect her. Protect her from men like Gable. "I cannot imagine your agony over having to return the boy in such a state."

"Yes, I believe you can imagine it, Lettie." He turned slightly to face her on the bench. "You lived my reality day after day for six years. Mine was a brief moment that changed my future in an instant. I cannot imagine the turmoil you are burdened with after so many years of tending the injured, watching men die on the battlefield, and holding soldiers as they expired under your care."

"Not all died. Many lived and returned to battle or were sent back to England." During all those years, she'd never stopped to think what the lasting burden would be on her soul. No thought had been given to what would happen when she returned to England when the war was over. She'd especially never dreamt of a future without Gregory at her side. Her husband had witnessed all the same horrors as she. Together, they could have worked through anything. The reality was, Gregory was gone. Lettie was left to deal with everything on her own now...and she was failing miserably.

"While I cannot imagine the extent to which that type of experience changes a person, I am here for you. I will listen whenever you want to talk. I can help you reconcile it all and move forward because, *damn it*," he growled, "Lettie, you have a long life ahead of you. I will not stand by while you wither and rot alone in the country or here in town. I cannot condone your chosen exile for transgressions that are not yours to bear."

Lettie wanted to believe him. Believe that he would stay by her side. Believe there was a way to work through the mounting burdens holding her down and making it hard to breathe. Believe that even though Gregory was gone, Daniel was here, and he would save her, repair her mind, and stop the terrifyingly tangible nightmares.

"You must find meaning in life again, find your passion, and hold tight to it." He placed a kiss to her forehead, his warm lips banishing her chill. "All these years, you've been my passion. My drive to continue even though I was lost. It only took that heartbreaking Christmastide morning at Gable's to realize it all. You are bravery and courage personified, Lettie. You were strong and daring when I was nothing but weak and into my vices. You left everything you knew and leapt feet-first into the unknown—both in love and life. Bloody hell, I want you to show me how to live like that."

Daniel tenderly kissed her again, trailing light pecks across her forehead and down her cheek, kissing away the tears she hadn't realized were falling. "I am none of those things, Daniel. I am a fraud."

"No, you are more authentic than I have ever been. When I was crushed by my father's death and embraced a path of self-destruction, leaving my betrothed behind, it was you who picked up the pieces and found love for yourself with Gregory. Love and a new future. It was that morning, after leaving Charlie's family I made the decision to change. Live a life worth remembering, not endless days in a stupor with hazy memories of women and parties I couldn't quite grasp."

She'd never thought that his rakish behavior was because he was hurting. "I wish I could have been there for you," she exhaled as his lips reached hers. What might have developed between them if she'd stopped to wonder the reasons behind Daniel going from her childhood friend to a man she didn't recognize—almost overnight. Things could have been different had she not punished him for sinking into a life of debauchery. They could have found companionship and love, as had always been their parents' intentions.

Instead, they'd each chosen vastly different paths.

Lettie had chosen love and hardship with Gregory, while Daniel had set his sights on exploring all the vices the London underworld had to offer a man with more money than he knew what to do with and scruples that were seriously compromised by suffering.

Neither of them could turn back time and make different choices. Though Lettie longed to know what could have been had they both been strong enough to pick each other up instead of pushing one another away.

Chapter Seventeen

Daniel had confessed the worst of his sins, and she hadn't pushed him away and fled the room. He'd bared his soul, and she hadn't flinched at the ugliness inside him.

He'd expected nothing less—this was Lettie. The girl he'd teased mercilessly due to her bleeding heart, her way of looking at every situation and seeing the best of it; the best of every person involved.

That woman was still in there…somewhere.

And she was fighting to get out.

But he needed to get her to see that. To realize that, yes, war had changed her, but it had not extinguished her goodness, her innocent way of looking at the world. It had only altered how she responded to life's many challenges.

Her experiences hadn't broken her—nor should she allow them to define her. She needed to focus all her pent-up pain and channel it into something good.

With that, Daniel was certain her healing would come.

It was the purpose he also longed to find.

"There is a certain weight lifted, an unburdening, when one speaks of what holds them down." He pressed another kiss to her lips, lighter than before, but holding so much more…hope. He hadn't felt so divested in years. Ripped wide before Lettie, and she hadn't turned away in fear or disgust. "Tell me what holds you down? What keeps you from breathing freely?"

Daniel pulled back, giving her space to think—and breathe.

For a brief moment, he sensed her pulling away and shutting him out again as she stared into the unlit hearth across the room.

She pulled her hand from his grasp, and his heart plummeted.

What was possible for him, may not be for Lettie. Could it be her wounds ran too deep?

Lettie clenched her fists on her lap and began to talk. Quietly at first, so low he had to strain to hear her. "No one can imagine the carnage, death, and loss of war. The worst part is that as time passes, it all becomes routine. The blood, the cries of pain, and the hardships all become normal. They fail to shock a person. It all becomes a part of life. It even becomes common to overlook the far-reaching consequences of a soldier's death. It is not only the loss of life, but also the damage it does to others. A mother and father lose a son. A wife loses her husband. A child loses his or her father. Entire families are left destitute."

"I can understand how this can happen," Daniel volunteered.

"I did not understand my loss of sensitivity until Gregory died, only saw myself as doing the tasks expected of me: bandaging the injured, stitching wounds, treating fevers. I worked tirelessly, doing all I could to make camp life easier for Gregory and the other soldiers. When there was no one to tend to, I washed and mended uniforms, and cooked meals. It was dawn to dusk labor, and sometimes late into the night." She paused, finally bringing her eyes back to his. "I became jaded by the sight of death and violence. The sound of cannons or musket fire no longer startled me. I could prepare an entire meal in the rain with the shouts of *charge* in the distance. By the time Gregory was wounded—and had died—I'd stopped fearing death was a possibility for him at all. He was invincible to me."

"I am so sorry, Lettie." Daniel leaned forward, placing a chaste kiss to her temple. "He was a brave man, far braver than I could ever hope to be."

She shook her head. "Just because a man is willing to die on a battlefield does not make him any more courageous than those who stay behind when their loved ones go to war." Her hands trembled, and she clutched her skirt. "All my work, all the heartache, and these families may never know the final resting place of their soldier. May never be given the closure I was lucky enough to have. They have no promise of anything to come to help raise their children, keep a dry roof over their heads and food on their tables."

"You cannot assume responsibility for all these people." However, it was exactly something Lettie would think to do.

"That does not stop the guilt of knowing I returned to London to a home, fine clothes, and a guaranteed future, no matter my husband is dead. My mother's title will still pass to me after her death. My family will always take care of me, even if I never collect the many pieces of myself. Even you...you are more than most war widows have: the simple support of a friend."

"Mayhap it is your destiny to fix that, at least for those needing you." It was the purpose she needed.

"My parents will never allow this." She hung her head in shame.

"Do you need their approval?" he asked. "Lettie, you were put on this earth to make it a better place. That is something they know."

"But giving to those less fortunate than us?" Lettie shook her head. "My mother believes in charitable work, but nothing that actually makes a difference. Knitting caps and mittens for children only does so much if the family's basic needs are not met. They will never agree to allow me access to my dowry if I only plan to give it away."

"Then let me help you." His hand lifted and settled against her cheek. He needed her to see the sincerity of his offer. "You can have all my money, everything I have, to start until they are convinced and allow you access to your dowry or you marry. And if the man is ignorant enough not to support your work, then you will continue to have control of my assets."

"You cannot mean that," she breathed. Her intense stare searched his face.

"But I do." And he wanted to be at her side during it all: helping her, guiding her, supporting her in any way he could. If she only needed him to lift heavy things or drive her about in his carriage, Daniel would do that. "Life must have purpose, and I believe your purpose is helping others. You tended the wounded, and now you can actively help women and children who've lost a loved one at war. I promise to do all in my power to aid you, be there for you like I should have been all those years ago."

"Do not say that, Daniel," she said in a steady, low-pitched voice with no hint of a tremble. "It was I who left you. Instead of trying to figure out what had sent you on a downward spiral, I met Gregory, married, and fled London; however, that does not mean I did not think of you often."

His hopes soared at her confession.

"I thought of you every day, Lettie." Blast it all, but it was the truth. There was no going back, no denying it any longer. "I've loved you since childhood. I loved you when I couldn't love myself. I agreed to end our betrothal *out of love* for you, and I blame myself every day for not fixing myself, pulling myself out the depression I was in, and claiming you as mine. When you left England, my reason for going on was gone. Any ounce of me that had longed to be a better person disappeared when you did. You are my past, my present, and my future. I had no future once you were gone. I was a boat left to drift at sea without the promise of rescue."

She pulled her hands from his grasp and leapt to her feet.

He'd bared his soul and there was nothing left to do but accept her reaction to his honesty. Daniel had no room left in his life for regrets.

Chapter Eighteen

Lettie stared into the flameless open hearth. No warmth would come from its eerily dark space. No answers would be found in its gaping expanse. There was no epiphany awaiting her. No guidance from above. She was alone in her decision.

Daniel loved her. Somewhere within her, a place so deep she'd have to focus far longer than she had in months to find it, she knew his words and his feelings were nothing but the truth and had been uttered in complete openness of heart.

What was not so easily understood was if she were capable of returning his affection. She'd left everything on the battlefield, and in that meadow at Waterloo. She'd left England a whole person, a woman who'd found her forever love in a man who understood her. However, she'd returned a broken widow, plagued by terrors that did not wait for the cover of darkness to attack.

Those same nightmares had changed since her return home. No longer did Gregory lay dying in her arms, but Daniel—his battered face and bruised body crushing her. An overwhelming sense of remorse filled her. Lettie led to nothing but heartbreak and suffering. Daniel needed to see this. She could not put him through that future, *her* future.

She'd betrayed all Gregory had been, all he'd given up, and all they had by even thinking of Daniel during those dreams. While the night terrors were rife with anguish, they were the only moments she could spend with Gregory…and Daniel had taken his place.

She should feel a traitor, a woman not worthy of the great love Gregory had given her—but she didn't. Not an ounce of her held any remorse for her wayward dreams.

Did that mean Lettie had more to give? Maybe she wasn't as shattered as she'd thought.

Even now, she thought more rationally than she had in months. Could focus and purpose be her saving grace? Or did her salvation lie in the arms—and heart—of Daniel?

Or, the most frightening notion, her mind was so far gone she could not accurately remember the past in a dream state.

She lifted her hands and pressed each to the sides of her face as her head pounded, threatening to scatter her musings and resolve once more. A thumping pulse increased behind both eyes. Her skin heated as if on fire.

It was all too much.

How could Daniel love a woman who couldn't even think long enough to reconcile simple ideas? She wasn't capable of making it through a dinner party without falling apart.

She had nothing to offer anyone. She'd lost any sense of who she was when she'd buried Gregory in that meadow. Where she was going and how she'd get there eluded her. Lettie couldn't risk taking Daniel down that long, dark path with her.

"Please, give me a chance," he pleaded, his tone sorrowful and laced with a desperation she'd never known he possessed. "Do not give up on me. On us."

"There is no *us*, Daniel. There is barely a *me*." She turned to face him, her hands falling limply at her sides. "How can you say you love me?"

"I do." His face was masked by the darkness of the room, but the certainty in his voice was unmistakable.

"You love the woman who left six years ago. You do not know the woman I've become. If you did, you'd likely run far from me." She crossed her arms across her chest, suddenly aware that her gown still hung open in the back and draped low in the front. She was bared to him both on the inside and the outside. "I am broken. I do not think love is something within my grasp. You may love me, but what if I am unable to return that affection?"

"Do we both not deserve a chance?"

"A chance at what?" Lettie argued. "You would be giving up a happy future for a woman who may never be capable of love. And I will become a burden to you. Our mutual discontent will fester with time…"

"You cannot know any of this." He stood and moved to stand in front of her, taking her hands in his. "I am not asking you to do this for me. I have never deserved someone as fine as you, Lettie. I'm begging you to do this for yourself. I would be content with a lifetime of loving you, no matter where your heart lies."

Daniel squeezed her hands where they warmed from his touch.

Lettie wished he could reach more than just her hands, but her heart constricted with ice more and more as the days passed and it slowly sent tendrils of frigid blood through her entire body—reaching every extremity.

He was offering her the world: security, adoration, love, acceptance, and the chance to piece back together the remnants of who she'd been so she could decide who she wanted to become. She'd spent so many years chasing Gregory's dream; putting her at risk in camp, exposing her to the cruelties of humanity, and baring her soul to a million heartbreaks. Never once did she realize his dream did not embody *her* dreams. She'd blindly followed him instead of finding her own path. It was far easier to believe she was doing good and making the correct choices as long as the choices never actually belonged to her. She'd never comprehended that there was another way to live.

Lettie had embarked on the journey of life with no hesitation.

She still held no regrets about that decision.

It was through sheer amounts of blood, sweat, and tears that she'd been lucky enough to return home. She'd dreamed of her homecoming during those long, cold nights. She'd longed to see her family once more, even Daniel. She'd fought hard to keep her wits about her during some of the most vicious battles.

Now, she was here, with Daniel, and all she could think of was the hardships she'd face while away from him, even while he offered her the opportunity to live her own dreams, unrestrained by others.

To find all the pieces of her and put them back together. Maybe not in perfect order, but into some semblance of the woman she used to be.

Lettie feared her mind would never work properly again. The thoughts rushing through her were like autumn leaves falling during a heavy wind, scattering to and fro with no concrete path or ultimate destination. Was she destined to live the rest of her life blown about, her course changing with the smallest breeze?

Daniel was offering her more than love. More than financial security. He was giving her the chance to grasp on to something stable and solid—unmoving. He would root her to the ground where she chose to be, and would never allow her to flounder at the mercy of others or her erratic mind. But for how long could he love her despite them both, knowing she wasn't exactly right and his love might never be returned?

She stared into his deep, black eyes, concern etched in the lines of his smooth face as he waited for her to work through whatever was happening within her. Lettie longed to run her fingers along his brow and remove his worry for her. No one had ever given her space and time to think through her actions. Truly, when her mind was sound and whole, she hadn't needed any extra time. She'd always been certain of the path she would take. Never had she needed anyone to guide her.

But now, she needed someone—*him*.

What would happen to her if he decided this was all too much for him to take on?

A quiver fluttered in her stomach at the thought.

"Lettie." Daniel kissed her forehead, and her eyes drifted shut. No one had ever treated her so tenderly. "I am broken, too. Mayhap not in the same ways as you, but I understand all that you've witnessed—death, violence, and loss. When you left, I tried to mask the pain of losing you with liquor, and surrounded myself with people who didn't care a whit for me. That way, if they left, I would not *feel* what I felt with you. Because of this, a boy lost his life. I am responsible for that. I will spend my life making amends for it. All those lost at war...that blood is not on your hands. Allow me to prove that to you."

Without taking his eyes from hers, he spread her hands wide, palms up. He leaned down and placed a kiss on each palm before gazing back at her.

"See, there is no blood. If anything, there are men who survived *because* of you. Families were reunited because of your quick thinking and medical aid. Men had clean clothes and full bellies because you cared enough about them all to work tirelessly, day in and day out."

Lettie looked down at her hands, calloused from years of labor. They were, indeed, without bloodstain. The hardship remained in the way of roughness, but no flakes of dirt or blood clung under her nails.

Was it possible to scrub away her memories—live her life, never forgetting all the people lost and injured, but finding some form of peace? She would never let Gregory's memory go, but she could remember him, honor him, without throwing away her second chance at happiness.

"Lettie, I love you," he pleaded. "I beg you to give us a chance. The worst that can come is a lifelong friendship. The best, we both find love, happiness, and fulfillment with one another. I will never stop trying to make you happy. I will never turn away from you, no matter where life leads us. I want you—and only you—at my side."

If she accepted, would she doom Daniel to an uncertain future? As much as she wanted to jump in, believe his words, and know he could help her…she could not fully put him at risk. What if her mind didn't improve and only continued to deteriorate? The time may come that she was not fit to be around anyone, especially Daniel and any family they may have together.

She searched his face for any sign of unease or hesitation. Any hint that he did not wholly mean all he promised because, if she accepted his offer and she was never able to recover her sound mind, then she would never forgive herself for dragging Daniel down with her.

Chapter Nineteen

"You are *my* only hope." Daniel caressed Lettie's hands, trying to rid them of the chill that had descended on the room. From her lost, faraway look, he suspected she was no longer in this room with him. Jealousy spiked at the thought of her in his arms but thinking of another man—or even another place. Could a man be envious of a *place*, especially a place that lay a far distance away? "Without you, I have no future."

"With me, you may not have one either. I am uncertain if I am capable of going on."

His stomach dropped with her declaration, and tendrils of ice coursed through him.

He didn't want to think about what he'd do if she pushed him away, told him not even a friendship could exist between them. It would be more than he could handle.

Lettie could survive years of camp life and hardship, but he couldn't even live past the rejection of a woman.

Not *a* woman.

His woman.

Lettie, Lady Colette Hughes, was the only woman he'd ever envisioned himself with. Wedding and starting a family with. Living in town or the country—hell, he'd move to Scotland if that's what she demanded of him. Anywhere she longed to be, he would follow. Any purpose in life she settled on, he would wholeheartedly support.

There was no other option for Daniel.

He loved her so entirely, without her, he'd have no will to go on. He would not sink back into his rakehell ways. No. He would simply cease to be.

"Tell me, Lettie, tell me you will at least try." His voice cracked on the final word.

"My heart wants all you offer." Lettie lowered her head. "However, my mind is unable to reconcile it all. Does the heart have the ability to love two men so entirely?"

His back stiffened and hope soared. "Are you saying you love me?"

She shook her head as if to banish her muddled thoughts and lifted her eyes to meet his once more. "Daniel, my heart has always loved you—it was my mind that wouldn't give in to the emotion, fearing your drinking and debauchery would rip my heart out and leave me destitute. However, I chose another…and here I am, still destitute."

Daniel saw the regret in her. "You did what you thought was right. I can never blame you for that. At the time, I was not prepared for a woman of your caliber. I likely would have hurt you."

"But you are different now?"

"Of course," he whispered. "I have realized my missteps, dealt with the loss of my father, and I know—without a doubt—that you are the woman I want by my side for eternity. If the eternity is spent in London, that is where we shall be. If you deem a life in the country suits you best, we will travel there. Hell, if you want to live on a schooner in the Atlantic Ocean, I will learn to swim and fish."

"The place is not important," she sighed. "A place cannot make me whole again."

"Then what, Lettie? What will make you whole again?" he demanded patiently.

"I do not know. I may never know, but because of you, I want to try." She ran her hands through her short hair and stood.

His heart soared. "What are you saying?" He needed her confirmation, to know she wanted him by her side to help her find herself once more.

She leaned in toward him, her hands reaching for his face and settling at his cheeks. She ran her fingers under his eyes and across to his temples. Daniel hadn't realized his head thumped in expectation. The headache receded as she caressed his face.

Finally, she smiled a tentative smile. Not weak—in no way was Lettie weak. She was the strongest person he'd ever known. "You may be lost now, but together, we can—no, we *will*—overcome this. I have no doubt of that."

She lifted on her tiptoes and set her mouth against his for a light, chaste kiss before stepping away. "I do not know if it is easy to overcome what holds my mind hostage, but…" Her words trailed off, and a soft sob left her.

Her mouth parted, and she drew her bottom lip in and nibbled on it.

"Nothing in life worth having comes easily," he said.

"Oh, Daniel, I want to try—with you," she confessed.

The words were all he needed to pull her back into his arms, everything else forgotten.

The gathering in the dining hall downstairs. The expectations for her parents. The future of her mother's estate. The watchful eye of society.

None of it mattered.

Lettie mattered, only Lettie.

And she was willing to give him the opportunity to love her. The chance he'd turned away from six years ago.

The future he would never take for granted again.

He loved her with his whole heart and mind.

She loved him with her heart—now, they only need convince her mind that it was capable of the same.

It would be a difficult, harrowing journey, but Lettie had seen and done worse. With her steel strength and him to guide her, there was no way they'd fail.

He pulled back far enough to lean down and kiss her and run his hand through her hair.

She pushed against him, her lips as demanding as his.

He allowed her control, gave her the power to take their kiss and embrace in whatever direction she longed to.

Not surprisingly, she wrapped her arms around him to caress his back, her fingers digging tightly into his waist to keep him securely to her as her tongue darted out and slowly crept along his bottom lip.

She tasted him, and Daniel wanted nothing more than to savor her in return.

The softness of her welcoming lips, as she hesitated for a brief moment before giving in to what Daniel knew she wanted—complete exploration of one another both emotionally and physically.

Daniel pulled back, needing to gaze into her eyes, make sure she understood and believed in his commitment to her—and their future together. "Lettie, I am here for you, *with* you. Every minute of every day I will stand devoted to you…and to us. Anything and everything you desire will be yours. I will make sure of it. I will love you until my last days on earth, and then, never fear, I will love you in the next world. I will live every day to make you happy."

"This, with you near, is when I think that healing is possible." She looked up at him, her eyes no longer holding the haze he'd noted since picking her up at The George. "It is because of you I also have hope—for myself and the future."

"Allow me to love you forever, Lettie."

"I will have it no other way."

Epilogue

London, England
Summer 1816

Lettie wiped the dusty rag across her forehead, causing her shoulder-length golden brown locks to fall into her eyes. Huffing, she tilted her head to send the strand back where it belonged. Not that things ever stayed where they belonged, at least not for Lettie.

"Allow me to help you." Daniel hurried across the room and righted the chair she'd been cleaning of dust and grime from years of disuse. "I told you to rest…and this is what you do?"

Correction, nothing stayed where they belonged but Daniel.

He'd followed through on every promise he'd made to her—and more which hadn't been spoken aloud that night in her bedchambers.

He'd been her rock, her footing when she sensed her mind slipping, her anchor when the waves threatened to wash her away, and through it all, he'd only loved her more, lavished more attention on her, and held her ever closer.

"I am with child, Daniel," she scolded. "I am not helpless or so advanced I will expire from a bit of hard work."

She softened the rebuff with a smile.

Lettie smiled all the time now and laughed with no remorse.

Odd how she'd lived for so many years without either, and now they came out of nowhere, overtaking her without warning. She awoke smiling, brushed her hair holding back a giggle as he demanded to assist her, and outright chuckled at Daniel's silly antics.

As she'd suspected, her parents were not willing to hand over her dowry to be used at Lettie's discretion; however, they'd readily agreed to a betrothal and spring wedding for her and Daniel. The deed was no sooner completed and her dowry given into Daniel's safekeeping than the funds were transferred into an account in only her name, as well as another healthy portion of funds. More funds than Lettie could conceive of means to dispose of.

Yet not a fortnight had passed, and Lettie had established a plan—with her husband's help.

Focus and purpose, as well as Daniel's unconditional love and support, were slowly but surely helping to heal her mind. He'd been right about that, though very wrong about another thing.

She was not his only hope…Daniel had been *her* only hope.

"Just sit down, I will finish in here." He pushed the chair she'd been working on behind her, and she sat.

It did feel heavenly to be off her feet, but there was so much more to do.

"Daniel, please, Deloris and her children will be here before the sun sets." She leaned forward in the chair, setting the palm of her hand against her growing belly, a barely noticeable flutter greeted her. "The children will need beds, and Deloris will need a warm, quiet room."

"Do not fret." Daniel glanced around the room. "We only have this space to worry about."

"Whatever are you saying?" Lettie sighed. "I haven't even begun on the children's room. I need to spread their new coverlets, fold the clothes we've collected for them, and stack their school books on their shelf."

They'd worked tirelessly since locating and purchasing Hope Manor to ready the rooms and create a welcoming environment for other women who'd lost their husbands to war. Any family was welcome to stay until they could properly care for themselves.

"It is all done."

"What do you mean, it is all done?" Her brow arched in question. "I have spent all morning in here."

"You were so focused you didn't hear me working in the next room?" he asked.

"I suppose I was working rather hard," Lettie conceded, glancing around the room that had slowly taken form. It had once been a salon of sorts, but now would house a woman in need. She may need silence or prefer to be surrounded by activity—whatever her individual needs, they would be met as best as Lettie could arrange.

"As you always do, my heart." He knelt before her, so much like another special night that had changed their entire future, merging their courses into one path. "Another reason I love you." He placed a quick kiss to her cheek as running footsteps sounded in the hall. "Oh, no, they've found us!"

Lettie swatted at his shoulder but accepted his offered hand to stand. She'd no more gained her feet when a little boy skidded across the threshold, bouncing with excitement.

"Is it time? Is it time?" his tiny voice screeched to the clap of his hands.

"Almost, my boy." Daniel moved across the room, ruffling the boy's mop of auburn hair as he passed. He collected the freshly laundered lilac blanket and moved to spread it across the bed.

"Deloris and her sons will be here before you know it, Owen." Lettie laughed as the boy hopped from one foot to the other. "Why are you so excited?"

"I'm the only boy here," he retorted, setting his hands on his tiny waist. "All these girls…they are trying my patience."

Daniel chortled, and Lettie turned a glare in his direction before smiling back at Owen. "It is certainly difficult being the only man in the house, I can see that."

"What about me?" Daniel called, his frown making Lettie laugh.

"You don't live here, your grace." Owen shook his head as if the weight of the entire household rested on him. "Anyways, it will be nice to have some boys to play marbles with or to play tricks on the girls."

Lettie and Daniel laughed. With only three families in residence at Hope Manor, Owen being the only boy, he was seriously outnumbered.

"Owen!" a woman shouted from down the corridor. "You get back here and finish your schoolwork. And for heaven's sake, leave the duke and duchess alone."

Owen winked and rushed back toward the door, stopping for one last word. "I do hope they hurry. This arithmetic and reciting are getting on my last nerve."

Daniel moved up behind Lettie, settling his arms around her waist and pulling her close. "Do you think our child will be so precocious?"

"With parents like us, Charlie is destined to be either a rascal or a hellion," she mumbled as he pressed his lips to her neck.

His mouth halted, and she felt him pull away. "Charlie?"

"Oh, I've meant to speak with you on the matter. I have selected a name."

"But what if we have a girl?" he asked.

"Charlie will still suit. It is a strong name, perfect for either a boy or a girl." The decision had been an easy one, far simpler than many she'd been pressed to make previously. "Are you upset?"

He spun her around in his arms, so quick her head swam, first from the sudden movement and then from the look of complete adoration and affection in his eyes.

Daniel had promised her a second chance at life, but she'd never dreamt she'd truly grasp hold of a second chance at love.

"My dear wife, I could not be any less upset." He bent slightly and caught her below the knees, lifting her into his arms. She nestled against his chest with a sigh. "Now, it is rest for you…and Charlie."

"But our new guests will be here shortly," she argued.

"Not for several hours." He pulled her tighter to him. "Just enough time to return home, sleep, and be back at Hope Manor refreshed and ready to greet our guests."

Daniel had been so kind since she'd concocted her harebrained idea for Hope Manor; a place for women and children to come while they healed from the loss of a loved one without fear of mounting debt, empty bellies, or hearths lacking coal.

"I suppose the least I can do is return home and rest, especially after you arranged the children's room." She laughed coyly. "I think perhaps you need a nap as much as I."

"It is not a nap I'm looking forward to." He waggled his brows, leaving no doubt in her mind that their afternoon of rest would likely not include sleep. "Now, I grow weak with exhaustion. Let us be off."

"I am ever at your command, your grace."

They both laughed. His unrestrained deep chuckle and her light giggle, as they both knew well and good it was Daniel who would always be at *her* command.

And that pleased them both greatly.

With Daniel at her side, the nightmares did not overtake her sleep as often, but when they did, he was there to kiss her awake and banish the horrors. Ever at her side and in her heart.

Thankfully, her mind had embraced his love, as well.

Books By Christina McKnight:

Lady Archer's Creed Series

Theodora (Book One)

Georgina (Book Two) – Coming 2017

Adeline (Book Three) – Coming 2017

Josephine (Book Four) – Coming 2017

Craven House Series

The Thief Steals Her Earl (Book One)

The Mistress Enchants Her Marquis (Book Two)

The Madame Catches Her Duke – Coming late 2017

The Gambler Wagers Her Baron – Coming 2018

A Lady Forsaken Series

Shunned No More, A Lady Forsaken (Book One)

Forgotten No More, A Lady Forsaken (Book Two)

Scorned Ever More, A Lady Forsaken (Book Three)

Christmas Ever More, A Lady Forsaken (Book Four)

Hidden No More, A Lady Forsaken (Book Five)

The Undaunted Debutantes Series

For The Love Of A Widow

The Disappearance of Lady Edith (Book One) –
Coming May 2017

The Misfortune of Lady Lucianna (Book Two) –
Coming June 2017

The Misadventures of Lady Ophelia (Book Three) –
Coming June 2017

Standalone Title

The Siege of Lady Aloria, A de Wolfe Pack Novella

A Kiss At Christmastide: Regency Romance Novella

For The Love Of A Widow: Regency Romance Novella

About the Author:

USA TODAY Bestselling Author Christina McKnight writes emotional and intricate Regency Romance with strong women and maverick heroes.

Her books combine romance and mystery, exploring themes of redemption and forgiveness. When not writing she enjoys coffee, wine, traveling the world, and watching television.

Email: Christina@ChristinaMcKnight.com
Follow her on Twitter: @CMcKnightWriter
Keep up to date on her releases:
www.christinamcknight.com
Like Christina's FB Author page:
ChristinaMcKnightWriter

Author's Notes

Thank you for reading *FOR THE LOVE OF A WIDOW*.

If you enjoyed *FOR THE LOVE OF A WIDOW*, be sure to write a brief review at any retailer.

I'd love to hear from you!

You can contact me at:
Christina@christinamcknight.com

Or write me at:
P O Box 1017
Patterson, CA 95363

www.ChristinaMcKnight.com
Check out my website for giveaways, book reviews, and information on my upcoming projects, or connect with me through social media at:

Twitter: @CMcKnightWriter

Facebook: www.facebook.com/christinamcknightwriter
Goodreads: www.goodreads.com/ChristinaMcKnight

Sign up for my newsletter here:
http://eepurl.com/VP1rP

There are several people I'd like to thank for staying with me through the emotional journey of writing this book.

To Marc, my amazing boyfriend—thank you for always being *you*!

To Lauren Stewart, my critique partner and best friend, you pushed me to explore new avenues of thought that I never dreamed possible. If we were in a true relationship, it would be one based on co-dependency, but in a good way. My writing would not be what it is without your comments, criticism, suggestions, and guidance.

I'd also like to thank the wonderful women who've supported me in both my writing career and life, including (but not limited to): Amanda Mariel, Debbie Haston, Angie Stanton, Theresa Baer, Erica Monroe, Ava Stone, Roxanne Stellmacher, Laura Cummings, Dawn Borbon, Suzi Parker, Jennifer Vella, Brandi Johnson, and Latisha Kahn. I know I'm forgetting people…You have all been very patient and wonderfully supportive of my eccentric ways.

A very special thank you to my editor, Chelle Olson with Literally Addicted to Detail, your skill and professionalism surpass all that I expected. Chelle Olson can be contracted by email at
literallyaddictedtodetail@yahoo.com.

Also, a special thank you to historical and developmental editor, Scott Moreland.

And to my proofreader, Anja with Hourglass Editing, thank you for embarking on yet another journey with me.

Cover and wraparound cover design and website design credit to Sweet 'N Spicy Designs.

Finally, thank you for supporting indie authors.

www.ingramcontent.com/pod-product-compliance
Lightning Source LLC
Chambersburg PA
CBHW021041130626
46552CB00005B/1965